THE BLACK HOTEL

Nightmar[illegible]alie thought. They co[illegible]

But sh[illegible]Donald, and dawn wa[illegible]

She cr[illegible]luish ecto-plasmic in[illegible]he stepped back as it f[illegible]

Seconds [illegible] darkness, she felt something brush past [illegible] She sensed a presence in front of her and behind her, neither more than three feet away, but invisible, and she slammed the door shut.

One of them, she felt, was in the room, but she turned and made straight for the telephone to call security.

The phone was dead.

Also by Andrew Laurance in *Star*

PREMONITIONS OF AN INHERITED MIND
THE LINK
THE EMBRYO
THE HISS
OUIJA

THE BLACK HOTEL

Andrew Laurance

Star

A STAR BOOK

Published by
the Paperback Division of
W. H. ALLEN & Co. Ltd

A Star Book
Published in 1983
by the Paperback Division of
W. H. Allen & Co. Ltd
A Howard and Wyndham Company
44 Hill Street, London W1X 8LB

Printed in Great Britain by
Hunt Barnard Printing Ltd, Aylesbury, Bucks

ISBN 0 352 31266 1

THE BLACK HOTEL

Hyde Park Gate. London.

5.30 on the morning of June 25th.

Natalie Weir came out of the Palace Plaza by the side entrance and crossed the road.

She stood on the pavement alone for a while, staring up at the towering magnificence of the new hotel, shining in all its glass and copper glory against the pale dawn sky. Then she gasped in horror as first one window panel shattered, then another, then another and misshapen human figures, like twisted rag dolls, were hurled out in the air to plummet helplessly down to the road below.

Eight victims in the space of a few seconds, impelled from different storeys by an unexplainable force to fearful death.

CHAPTER ONE

As she walked up the five wide marble steps to the revolving doors, she was saluted by the doorman in his black uniform with its gold trimmings and his black top hat with gold cockade.

Once inside, when she found herself in the palatial reception foyer, all glass, brass and marble, she felt she had made a mistake in coming at all.

This was elegant luxury. This was how the rich lived, not her. It had been madness to ring up in answer to the advertisement.

Now that she was here however, and expected, she would have to go through with it.

Nerves or no nerves.

'My name is Natalie Weir,' she said to the receptionist, 'I have an appointment at twelve noon with the manager, Mr Martineau.'

She looked up to check the time. The hotel clock itself was a work of art, gold encrusted hands and figures in the shape of branches and leaves set into a black marble façia.

It was exactly twelve o'clock. She had been to some lengths to arrive absolutely on the dot, had in fact waited outside for two minutes studying the new and controversial building.

'Mr Martineau will be with you presently. Would you care to take a seat?' the receptionist said, putting his phone down and indicating a seating area round a small delicate fountain.

She smiled and walked across the dove grey carpet, sinking in glorious comfort into one of the black velvet upholstered seats.

She looked at her surroundings. It would of course be quite extraordinary if she got the job. Quite extraordinary and quite incredible.

To be at the heart of such an empire would be revolutionary as far as she was concerned. Imagine living permanently in this atmosphere, all the staff at your beck and call, apart from the salary they were offering!

She thought of lighting a cigarette, then decided against it. She might be too nervous to hold it steadily.

She went over in her mind all the information she thought would be essential for the interview, pleased now that she had done her homework.

Opened three months earlier on June 15th, the London Palace Plaza was the newest hotel in the Euro-International Group, which owned twenty-three other hotels in the world, this the first in England. With four hundred and twenty-five rooms and suites, all with private bathrooms, shower, radio, colour television and direct dial telephone, it also had three restaurants, four bars, three suites for conferences, receptions, banquets, dinner dances and exhibitions, a swimming pool, a sauna, a chapel and an underground car park.

She glanced at her watch, at the clock again, picked a speck of something white off her beige pencil slim skirt. At least she had been wise enough to wear the suit once before today so that it didn't look as though it was bought for the occasion.

Her short, well-cut blonde hair always looked tidy, she knew, her nails were in good condition, her brown shoes perfect, from a presentation point of view she couldn't fault herself. All that she was nervous about was answering questions regarding the type of guests such a hotel would have. She had been in Public Relations for five years, had worked for one of the best Anglo-American agencies for four of those, but it had been a desk job, mainly writing proposals and dealing with two clients, one a shoe manufacturer, the other a chain of restaurants. Admittedly she had learned a good deal about catering through them, but they had hardly been in this class. They had, to say the least, been rather down market.

She needed a change, wanted a change, and was determined to get a new job. With this one, however, she might be biting off more than she could chew.

She guessed the tall brunette with bouncing hair and the practised smile coming towards her was either Mr Martineau's secretary or Vivien Brooks, head of PR, to whom she had spoken on the phone to make the appointment.

'Miss Weir? I'm Vivien. Mr Martineau will see you now.'

They made polite banal conversation all the way to the all copper lifts, then went silently up to the first floor and down a short dark carpeted corridor to a quiet spacious office.

It had a low ceiling, diffused daylight from behind venetian blinds, a half moon desk, luxury plus as everywhere else, and a deep too-comfortable chair to sit in.

A cigarette? A drink?

'A vodka and tonic please . . .' Vivien studied her as she was pouring out the drinks. Mr Martineau, tallish, elegant, grey haired, handsome with healthy tan, could have been a hotel guest himself.

They probably slept together, Vivien and Martineau, and her getting the job would either depend on him fancying her or her not being such a threat to the 'lady'. Sleeping with him wouldn't be terrible. She was aware that such jobs weren't only won because you had a good brain or an efficient mind. You had to have those *as well.*

Mr Martineau glanced down at something on his desk, presumably her letter to him.

'You're at present with Marston Fields?'

'Yes.'

'And you've been there four years?'

'Yes, that's right.'

Such a tightness in the throat. The whole point was that she should not be nervous. PR people were so used to handling other people that they should never be nervous. Relationships were their business.

'You're an Accounts Executive and you've been handling the Dubb Steak House chain and K.W. Shoes?'

'Yes.'

'Happy doing that?'

She smiled. The first trick question, or no trick question at all, but just wanting to hear her talk.

'It's not very stimulating. It doesn't bring me into contact enough with other people.'

Wrong!

Blunder number one. Admitting that she didn't handle people.

'You haven't much experience liaising directly with the public?'

He was sharp, astute. She would have to be careful.

'Not in great quantities, no, though K.W. do employ nine hundred people here and in the States and I was in charge of U.K. staff problems.'

'So you do have experience of personnel?'

'Yes. I can claim to be the successful behind-the-scenes mediator in the 1981 strike which was reported in the Press, if you remember.'

'I don't, but I'll take your word for it.' He looked down to study her letter again. 'You mention here that you have many contacts with the Press. Can you expand on that?'

She ran off her list of personal friends in Fleet Street, journalists and TV people, which always impressed. She had met them through Felix, who she had recently broken up with. The real reason, if truth be known, was that she wanted to live and work in a community and not be alone in her flat every evening waiting for the phone to ring to be asked out to dinner on her expense account.

'Can you tell us a little bit about yourself?' Vivien asked.

Vivien was all legs, long fingers, long nails, a gash of a mouth with plenty of lipstick. Not quite sophisticated enough to compete with richer clients, but nearly. Style anyway; lots of style which was more than she herself had.

'Do you want a potted history? It's lasted for twenty-four years.'

'You look younger,' Mr Martineau said.

'Thank you. It has its disadvantages but I can look older if necessary.'

'I think you look very attractive as you are,' Mr Martineau said with ease. Flattery came easily to him, he was used to handing it out, and she took it graciously.

Score ten for aplomb, she thought.

'I was born in Chichester, Sussex, educated at Inglefield School for Girls, went to the Sorbonne for two years reading Philosophy, but really to polish up my French which I speak fluently. I also speak a little Spanish and enough Italian to get by on the phone.'

'Have you travelled?'

'Most of Europe, Egypt and the States. Not South America, nor the East.'

'Interests? Hobbies?'

'Not really. I'm a workaholic. People I suppose. I do like people.'

'What do you think your duties would be here?' Martineau asked.

'Promoting the hotel and company's image, smoothing over any problems between guests and staff, organizing exhibitions, banquets, parties, and possibly looking after VIPs. Generally assisting Miss Brooks.'

'Did you know that you came with a very good personal recommendation?' Martineau asked her.

She sat up surprised.

'No.'

'The President of your company, no less. He's a friend of mine, always stays at whatever hotel I happen to be managing whenever he comes over from the States.'

'I hardly know him,' she said.

'He seems to know about you. Said you would be ideal, and I think he's right.'

He looked over at Vivien who nodded agreement, clinking the ice cubes in her long drink.

'When could you start?'

'Two months' notice would be expected.'

'We'd like you to settle in before Christmas when Vivien will need a lot of help.'

'If the President recommended me . . .' she started.

'He could no doubt see to it that you are allowed to go

sooner? I'll have a word with him. It's surprising what a chat in high places can do.'

'I know,' she said, smiling.

'Have *you* any questions?' Martineau asked.

She was ready for that. Phase two. Her demands. She hadn't expected to get this far, but was prepared.

'Other than salary, living accommodation, office accommodation, hours of work and holidays, no,' she said with some humour and new confidence.

'Vivien will cope with all that.'

He stood up, she stood up, he put out his hand, she shook it, and he said something about 'Welcome aboard' as Vivien opened the door for her. The VIP treatment it seemed, maybe so that she would know what others would expect from her.

The Public Relations office, a few doors down from Martineau's, was unbelievably untidy and housed two assistants: Bob who was Vivien's secretary and Tania who was a copywriter.

Bob was a trifle too slight to be regarded as manly, and Natalie sensed that she was older than him. Tania was probably in her mid-thirties, plumpish, displaying fat arms in the wrong sort of blouse for her shape. She also noted that there were dead flowers in a vase on the crowded window sill, files everywhere and that during the short space of time she was in the room three telephones rang at the same time, one of which went unanswered. It was a busy office, possibly to the point of inefficiency, which was why someone else was needed.

Inside Vivien's office the layout was similar to Martineau's but smaller and untidier. Vivien offered her another drink.

So to the all important questions.

All meals would be free, laundry free, everything personal free, and her salary would go up by six hundred a year. She would have the use of Tania as assistant and Bob when essential, but also could call on assistant managers, restaurant managers, banqueting managers, room service managers and anyone else who might prove useful in specialized areas.

A younger girl then walked in, smart, tall, blonde like herself, with a nervous smile.

'This is Sally,' Vivien said, 'My Number Two whom you are replacing. She'll show you around.'

Natalie got up and shook hands.

She left her drink on the desk and followed Sally out after an introductory chat.

'I'll show you to my own room first, the quarters you'll be escaping to, then the main areas of the hotel.'

They walked down the corridor and through a fire escape door, across the concrete landing of some back stairs where it was quite cold.

'This,' Sally said, 'is as near as I ever get to leaving the hotel. I've sometimes not gone out for a week. There are disadvantages living on the premises and though no one's supposed to bother you during your official time off, they're pretty quick to get you on the phone when something goes wrong . . . like a guest with chronic appendicitis when Sister's off, which happened last night!'

They went through another fire escape door and down a warm, carpeted corridor and stopped outside one of the many doors.

Sally took a key from her pocket.

'Security have a pass-key, but there is a double lock on the inside room should you ever feel you're in danger from one of the managers.'

'Are the managers dangerous?'

'Five out of ten. The rest are gay.'

It was a very small suite with an excuse of a living room dominated by a brand new bicycle leaning against the sofa.

'A gift from one of my admirers,' Sally said. 'We had a cycle sports exhibition here and I got given one. You get a lot of perks if you're nice to the clients.'

'How nice?'

'I earned the bicycle. But this was an outright generous gift, absolutely free,' she said, indicating a silver jug. 'Worth its own weight in silver, I'm told. Always useful for pawning.'

The bedroom was neat, with a large double bed, fitted

cupboards, a television set, and well equipped bathroom off.

Natalie looked out of the window which gave onto the back courtyard, staff car park and dustbins.

'There's double glazing so the noise isn't too bad,' Sally said. 'I never look out anyway.'

'Why are you leaving?' Natalie asked.

'I'm thinking of marrying a millionaire. That's another perk. You can pick them up here if you keep your wits about you. They're lazy and usually rather old. Mine has a little villa in Barbados. Ten bedrooms and two swimming pools.'

Next Sally showed her behind the scenes of one floor, the Panorama Restaurant on the eighteenth floor with its unique, all round views of London, its bar and its little dance floor.

They went to two of the banqueting suites on the second floor used for conferences and exhibitions, down to the swimming pool on the lower ground floor, and had a quick look at the vast kitchens which were right then a hive of noisy activity.

After that she returned to Vivien's office to finish her drink, and left with the promise that an official letter of confirmation and contract would be sent her.

Nobody is indispensable.

Natalie found that out the day after she gave in her notice at Marston Fields.

Noises were made in her direction about needing her office for someone else now that she was leaving, that her secretary could be better employed working for someone else now that she was leaving, and a hint was dropped that if she wanted she could have the holiday owed her and not bother to come back.

PR companies got nervous about departing executives and severences were usually swift and clean cut. So she left within the week as soon as she knew who was being promoted in her place – her own assistant whom she thought pretty useless.

She would have been depressed had she been going to a less luxurious job, but she still could not believe her luck, and though she tried to find out how and when the president had said complimentary things about her, she was never able to contact him and, aware that it might have been an entirely personal word with Martineau, she let it drop, thankful that it had happened at all.

The letter confirming her appointment as Assistant PRO at the London Palace Plaza Hotel for the Euro-International Hotel Corporation arrived promptly and she answered it just as promptly. After that she busied herself packing up her own small flat in Baron's Court which she decided to let to a friend on a temporary basis, not wanting to give it up as the lease was to run for another five years and she might well find the need to escape to a home of her own when the novelty and excitement of living in the hotel wore off.

She could have gone abroad for her holiday and it might have done her some good to have a complete change, but there was too much to be done and anyway she felt that going to live permanently in a luxurious hotel would seem like a holiday in itself.

Instead she went to stay with her mother, who lived a singularly simple life in a pretty little cottage near Chichester, caring for her garden, her dog and two cats.

Natalie did not really remember her father, an army officer who had died of heart failure when she was seven. His death ended an embarrassing family feud and had severed all connections with her paternal relatives.

Supposedly of aristocratic stock, he had made the unforgivable error of marrying below his station, eloping with one of the maids, her mother, who had learned the art of behaving like the upper classes so well that no one dreamed she came from such humble beginnings. It was only the tell-tale need to work for others that gave her away, an inborn servility which she herself inherited. What appalled Natalie was that her father's brother and sister had never contacted her after his death, but then that was because her grandparents had died leaving the so-called family fortune in a terrible mess and everyone connected had been bankrupted by the resulting death duties.

Families! She had not been very lucky. Her mother also

had been an only child and her parents had died long ago so that there were no relatives on that side, so school to her had been home, and school friends her sisters, until she had gone out into the world and suffered the pangs of young romantic love, and the distresses fired by the male desire for her young body.

She had eventually fallen in love, deeply enough to hurt her when it went wrong: unfaithfulness, deception, another girl. He swore it didn't mean anything, that he didn't understand why he had done it, but it had caused a rift and made her tougher and more determined to succeed on her own.

A humorous young man, her mother had called him, with a razor sharp wit that could cut deeply on occasions, and a serious turn of mind when it was necessary. She had been flattered that he had taken notice of her at all, he was a journalist and gossip columnist, he had introduced her to so many important people. But he didn't have a heart, or if he did it didn't seem to be in the right place.

Felix!

Their paths would cross again now no doubt. He had frequented the Ritz and the Dorchester, the Savoy and the Inn on the Park. If the Palace Plaza became as fashionable, he would be around, snooping for gossip.

Maybe he would need her one day, again.

On October 1st Natalie arrived at the London Palace Plaza Hotel in a taxi from Victoria station with her two suitcases of clothes, toiletries and a few books, deciding that whatever else she needed for her new life she would buy new.

She had arranged with Vivien that she would first arrive incognito as a hotel guest for three days so that she could get to know how the hotel worked from the client's point of view and make notes of what she thought was wrong and what she thought could be put right before the staff got to know her.

The taxi drew up, the doorman opened the door, and she went up the marble steps while a porter took her luggage and she checked in at reception.

She was taken to the seventh floor, Room 714, not the

best, but still luxurious, with a view looking west over Palace Gate Terrace and the Kensington rooftops. She unpacked one of her suitcases, the other containing possessions she would not need till she had settled into her own quarters.

The architects for Euro-International had clearly made the most of the expensive site, packing the four hundred and twenty-five rooms on eighteen of the low ceilinged floors, but taking up space for the entrance and reception rooms to give it grandeur. Everything had been carefully thought out, from air conditioning switches to the television set into the wall opposite the bed. The bathroom was neat with everything on hand and within reach from a position in front of the washbasin, and for the moment she could fault nothing.

A holiday in London!

She rang her mother to have a chat, then went downstairs to browse at the kiosks, the flower shop, the bookshop, the very expensive boutique concessions, then went out to a cinema knowing that once she was on duty she would probably find it hard to get time off for such entertainment.

Over the next two days she ate in each of the three restaurants and drank in all four bars, she got friendly with some Americans and got invited to a twenty-first birthday party. She danced in the Panorama Room, swam in the swimming pool, and on the Sunday morning even attended a short service in the hotel chapel.

Then, on October 4th she had her belongings moved down six floors to her own suite which was to be her home, and settled in.

Dressed more formally in a two-piece grey suit, she reported to Vivien in the PR office and was given her first job, the organising of the ninth Annual Jewellery Designers' Fair which Martineau had managed to wrestle away from another hotel, It therefore had to be successful.

The Suzerain Suite was designated and Bob was to help her.

The Suite would be closed on the Friday night for the stands to be built over the week-end, and the various clients would come in on the Sunday and Monday to open on the Tuesday at 10.00 a.m. It was a security problem more than anything else, and she would have to liaise with the house detective, Derek Edgars, a surly man who apparently saw nothing but evil in everybody.

Her main responsibility was to get to know each and every jeweller who was exhibiting, the assistants who would be at the stands, and make absolutely sure that she knew who their important customers would be. Fourteen rooms were booked for private entertainment, and she had the bright idea of booking them on a different floor so that rivals would not meet each other with clients, a subtlety that Vivien thought was quite unnecessary. The hotel was busy enough without such complications, the best attitude to adopt in order to be successful and survive oneself was that nobody, nobody at all, whether royalty or millionaire, was ever that important. If they didn't like it, they would have to lump it, the only person that really mattered was the man who hired and fired, and that was Martineau, and above him the big white chief Victor Krieselman, who might appear totally unexpectedly. Vivian kept a photograph of him in the centre drawer of her desk as he sometimes liked to disguise himself and appear with or without a moustache. He had once been known to wear a wig when visiting one of the company's hotels in Rome, but had never gone as far as using stilts, though he was rather short.

Three days into the Jewellery Fair, everything was going well. She received compliments from Vivien, but exhaustion was setting in because she was staying up till two every morning.

One of the joys of the hotel was the heating and air conditioning system which worked so perfectly that by regulating the temperature at night she could sleep naked under just the top sheet.

She'd just slipped herself between the cleanest of clean white sheets when the telephone rang and security asked her if she could possibly come to the Suzerain Suite.

'A problem?'

'Yes . . . but not over the phone.'

The thing was to remain calm, cool and collected. Even if that much publicized and grotesque diamond brooch designed by a mad Italian artist had been stolen she had to make absolutely sure the Press didn't hear about it.

She dressed quickly, put on a little make-up, as she could never be sure whom she might meet in a corridor, and went up to the Suzerain.

Derek Edgars, with his sullen face and balding head, was waiting for her as she crossed the brown and black check carpet. He was, as always, dressed in a charcoal grey suit, white shirt and green tie. With him were two security guards in dark blue uniforms and caps.

The centre showcase, she could see as she came in, had been smashed, though nothing of value had been left in any of the display units once the fair was closed for the night.

'Some bright spark tried to ease the top off,' Edgars said.

'When?'

'Between eleven and twelve.'

'Was there anything in it?'

'No.'

'So why?'

'A try out, I expect. Not necessarily for this exhibition, but maybe for the next somewhere else. The thing is,' he said, concerned, 'can you get it replaced before the morning without telling the client?'

'Did the alarm system work?' she asked.

'Yes.'

'Anyone caught?'

'No.'

'A mystery then?'

'A mystery.'

Derek Edgars clearly did not like unsolved mysteries, even less those that hinted at his security system being less than perfect and, for her part, the last thing she wanted was other clients panicking on hearing that it might be a try-on.

'Why don't you come up to the office and have a night cap?' she suggested.

She sat down behind Sally's old desk, pulled open a drawer and brought out the half empty bottle of brandy she'd found there 'for medicinal purposes' and other emergencies.

Cheering up the house detective was definitely an emergency.

'If the alarm worked, is it such a problem?' she asked.

'It worked so well that it'll spread a great deal of alarm everywhere. I've been in this business long enough to know that we must come up with a good story very quickly.'

'How else could the glass have been broken?' she asked.

'I could say that one of my men was testing it.'

'A security officer broke it?' It didn't sound too good to her. 'In which case we're responsible and have to foot the bill.'

Edgars nodded, biting his lip.

'It'll be paid for by the insurance people eventually, but the story will have to be proved,' he said.

'Which would mean someone taking the rap as scapegoat?' He tried a smile.

Well this was certainly an example of how experience and time in the business would have proved useful. She didn't know any of the staff well enough to judge who might be happy to take a little back hander for taking the blame. Vivien would probably know, but Vivien was at her own home away from the hotel and she could not be disturbed on such occasions.

So it was up to her.

She went to a filing cabinet in Vivien's office and found the staff file. She looked down the list of names for those who were on night duty and would have any reason to be in the Suzerain Suite.

The only one who fitted the bill was the chief engineer, or one of his assistants.

She told Edgars she'd be back soon, meanwhile to help himself to another brandy if he wanted.

She took the lift down to the basement where it smelt of diesel oil. Another world, of conduits and wires, cylinders and gauges, all remarkably clean, but then the hotel was new.

In the boiler room, where it was unbearably hot and the green, red, yellow and blue painted pipes made it look like the Pompidou Centre in Paris, she found two men each reading a newspaper in a small office.

'Good evening,' she said.

One stood up, the other didn't.

'I'm looking for Mr Grant.'

Grant was the one who hadn't stood up. He was in his early thirties, had curly ginger hair, a curly ginger beard and looked at her as though he regarded all women as bed objects.

He, she decided, was her man.

'I'm in trouble,' she said.

Grant raised an eyebrow, the weaker man looked concerned.

'There's a strong acrid smell coming from my air conditioning unit and one guest has complained. We don't want a Legionnaires' disease scare, so I wonder if you could find out what the problem is? My name is Natalie Weir, by the way, I work in the PR office.'

If Grant had wanted to look more truculent he would have had to try really hard.

'I'll come up and see,' the other man said, smiling.

She gave Grant a look of disappointment, and he moved quickly enough. Instant judgment had served her in the past. She didn't like the man's attitude and she wouldn't allow him to make demands, but physically there was something powerfully earthy about him and right now her feminine charm had to work.

'Best leave it to me, Ken,' Grant said. 'Environment is my domain, as they say. I'll wash my hands, if you can wait a minute, Miss?'

She waited a minute while Grant disappeared into a washroom, then followed him to the lifts when he came out.

He was gentlemanly enough to let her in first and when they were alone in the imposed closeness, he looked her over, smiling and nodding his head approvingly.

She wanted to slap his face, but instead she smiled herself. 'The air conditioning is working fine,' she said. 'It was an excuse.'

'I'd figured as much, but I've never seen you before.'

He was conceited, so arrogant that she wondered whether

women actually picked him up like this, whether such an encounter was part of normal life for him.

'Does this happen to you often?' she asked.

'Often enough. But they're usually older than you and ask me to come up in the morning when their husbands are out doing business.'

'I'm going to disappoint you. I don't want you for what you think,' she said.

He shrugged his shoulders.

'Gain one, lose one, doesn't matter to me.'

'But there is money in what I'm going to propose.'

On the first floor she led the way to her office. Edgars had gone, which didn't help. She gave Grant a glass of brandy and explained the situation.

She made it personal, explained her position, asked him how much he'd want to take the blame for breaking the showcase as far as the client and insurance people and management were concerned, until the jewellery fair was over.

He listened, incredibly cool, so cool that she wondered why a man with so much reserve was employed in such an uncomfortable job.

'I don't want money,' he said, 'but you can do me a favour. Get rid of Ken, my assistant. He's a right pain. I've got no power to sack him, he was sort of handed to me, but he really is no good.'

'Can you prove that?'

'No. He's a reasonable worker, but I have to live with him and we don't share the same interests. He's a bible thumper for one thing, and that can create a lot of irritations when you're a free-living soul like myself.'

'Have you anyone in mind as a replacement?'

'I've a mate who'd like the job.'

'I'll do what I can. In fact I promise I'll take care of it, but it may take a week or two.'

'That's all right, Natalie. So show me the case and I'll play the part of the lunatic who broke it.'

The following morning she put a call through to the

showcase people who said they would send someone over immediately. She talked to the managing director of the jewelry company explaining what had happened, and by ten o'clock, a few minutes after the exhibition opened, all was ship-shape, the jewellers were not even interested in how the damage had been done.

No one knew anything about the problem, therefore, except Edgars and Grant, and apart from making a note to have Grant's assistant shifted as soon as possible, the incident was closed until the insurance claim had to be signed. Her first test had been passed – she'd used discretion and tact.

It was just a fraction before noon when she went upstairs to check that all was well in the Panorama Bar for a small party being given by a publisher for the launching of a new travel guide. As she went in through the glass swing doors she was surprised to see one of the hotel guests sitting at the bar, which was supposed to be closed.

He was an elderly man, extremely thin, with a long face and bony bald head, and blue skin around deep sunken eyes. He was very pale, with long sinewy hands. His black suit was made of some strange shiny material that at one moment seemed transparent, and as she approached him, all smiles, she noticed that he was toying with an empty champagne glass.

'I'm awfully sorry,' she started,'but this bar is closed for a private function.'

The man looked her up and down and grinned, all knowing, amused by her concern.

'There are four other bars open,' she said.

He just stared at her and grinned.

It worried her. She felt that perhaps he was such a senile old customer that she might have trouble with him. Perhaps he had wandered up here by himself and was lost, but didn't even realize it.

'Are you staying in the hotel, sir?' she asked.

He grinned even more broadly as though this were an extremely funny question, then nodded his head several times and went on nodding.

'What is your room number?'

With her luck it would be one of the most expensive suites and he would turn out to be a VIP in the jewellery business.

But he didn't answer.

He just grinned and went on nodding his head as though approving of the way she was dealing with the problem he was setting her.

She looked around the room which was ready for the party. The cocktail snacks were on the tables, the publisher's display board was set up in a corner next to a counter piled high with copies of the new travel guide.

She went behind the bar and through the door leading to the staff area where the glasses and extra stock were kept. Steve, the barman, as professional as they came, was uncorking a number of wine bottles and she asked him who the old man was.

'What old man, love?'

He came back into the bar with her and there was no one in the room, which was an instant relief.

Just to make sure she looked around the restaurant, even behind the curtains, and went a little way down the corridor to see where he could have got to, but then forgot about him when the lift doors opened and a number of people from the publishing house stepped out and she introduced herself, led them to the bar and made sure that they had everything they wanted.

Downstairs in her office she found Sally sitting in her chair smoking a cigarette and toying with a drink.

'Don't tell me you want your job back?'

'No, I'm here as a customer,' Sally said. 'I'm leaving this green and pleasant land in two weeks and want to throw a party for all my friends, some of whom are staff here. Do you think Martineau would give me a special price?'

'If you choose a convenient date. The Sovereign Suite is pretty free.'

'I'm not too fond of the Sovereign. I was thinking of having a party in the Panorama with dancing. Most of my mates are in the band and it would be more fun.'

'Then it's just a matter of booking a large table and getting a discount on the menu and wine. How many would be coming, and when?'

'Fifteen, maybe sixteen, one day next week?'

'I'll see what I can do.'

'How are you liking it here?' Sally asked. 'Any problems?'

'No, nearly, but no. There was a funny old man up in the Panorama just now whom I thought would never leave.'

'Oh, him,' Sally said.

'Is he a resident, or something?'

'Sort of . . .'

'A regular then?'

'He's certainly a regular.'

'You're talking in riddles, Sally. Who is he? Not Krieselman the great white chief surely?'

To her surprise Sally got up and closed the door.

'No one knows who he is, and only a few people have seen him. Me, one of the room service managers and one of the women cleaners.'

'I still don't understand.'

'Well, don't take this too seriously, Natalie, on the other hand don't write it off as impossible either, but I think he's a ghost.'

'You're joking!'

'It's so far from a joke, between you and me, that he's the reason I gave in my notice. He came into my bedroom one night you see, stark naked, and stood at the foot of my bed, grinning. He didn't say anything, didn't do anything, but just stood there, playing with his limp self. Then he disappeared, and when I checked how he could have got in, it made no sense at all. The door was locked from the inside, and my room, then, was on the seventeenth floor.'

CHAPTER TWO

She had a conference with Vivien, her second month in.

'Your next job, and this is urgent, is to come up with something nobody else has so far been able to crack. We've been open just over five months now and haven't managed to grab the attention of the world, and I mean *the world.* We're an international hotel and, whereas the Connaught, the Ritz, the Savoy, the Hilton, and George V in Paris are continually in the news, we haven't yet got an image. We're not getting any free publicity and we should be. Your brief is to come up with an idea which will put the London Palace Plaza on the map. Points to note, however, are that we don't want to alienate non-show business people by becoming a movie star club, that's not our image, and we don't want to get mixed up with international political figures because that's dangerous. Hotels must sit on the fence, so we need a person who is newsworthy or an event that gets attention without either giving us the wrong image or an unrespected name.'

Natalie had expected to be landed with something impossible sooner or later, but all the same she looked upon this brief as a challenge. She went to her office, ordering all the papers and magazines world wide available from the newspaper kiosk and asked Tania to read through half the pile to check out which were worth reading, especially the gossip columns, and to write down all the names that made the news repeatedly.

It was a chance glance at the London evening paper that brought up a lead on someone no one had thought about. The name was very familiar and could well prove the answer to the problem. It rated seven lines on the front page anyway and the man was well known enough to be considered a household name.

> CARMEL DREIHARDT, American evangelist, is to visit London in the New Year. Wembley Stadium has been booked for two nights where he expects to convert thousands of British Christians to Genisism. The Genisists are a religious sect originating in the Arizona desert, who seek direct communication with God through intense individual prayer.

She picked up the phone and asked Tania to chase up all information on the Genisists and Dreihardt himself.

It took the whole of the next day to research, but she came up with something looking pretty good. The Genisists were apparently basically humanists and Dreihardt preached release from ecclesiastical authority and the liberation of the intellect to be as one with God, without religious trappings, but believing that freedom and happiness of others, justice and tolerance to others was to be uppermost in the minds of men at all times.

In a back number of *Time* magazine she found a whole article on Dreihardt, a man in his early sixties of Mormon parentage who had been a successful teacher of philosophy until his outstanding personality and preaching ability had attracted such a large following that he had channelled his ideas into a workable credo for the masses. He was a good man, respected by other religious leaders and had no political affiliations.

Natalie wrote out a succinct report for the hotel's board of directors, proposing that Dreihardt and his team of eight should be invited to stay at the hotel free during their four-day stay in London. The commercial and publicity advantages to be gained were a guaranteed massive media coverage of his visit – therefore a guaranteed mention of his London head-quarters (the Palace Plaza) without show biz or political overtones.

She read her proposal through to Tania who thought it excellent, took it to Vivien who thought it fantastic. She in turn took it to Martineau who congratulated Natalie on coming up trumps, and said he would put it in front of the board immediately. Speed, he was aware, was of the essence for, if everyone agreed to the plan, then Dreihardt would have to be wooed to accept the invitation which he would know was not entirely without commercial interests. And that could take time.

The go-ahead from the top came through very quickly, however, and Natalie was given *carte blanche* to do whatever had to be done for her proposal to succeed. So she made telephone calls and wrote letters and set the wheels of a stimulating public relations operation into motion.

She was happy, enjoying her work, and even more enjoying her new home.

It had happened once before in her life, what she called the 'root' feeling. Strangely enough it had been in a flat not far from the hotel, further up the road just off Kensington High Street behind Barkers in Wright's Lane. It was the first London flat she had shared and moved into and the moment she had set foot in the house itself she had felt at home as nowhere else.

It was an old house with creaking stairs up to the fourth floor flat and an awkward door opening outwards to what had once been the maid's quarters. Inside it was cosy, though the kitchen doubled as a bathroom with the old bath covered by a large board that flapped down onto it serving as a table.

The views from the dormer windows were of roofs and television aerials and other people's bedrooms and she had stayed there with her friend for two years, till both had done better and been able to afford to live on their own.

Home, true home, was Chichester, she supposed, but it had never had the same feeling. And now she was sensing it again, in this hotel. Just walking into the main reception foyer from the street, or even going into the place by the staff entrance at the back, made her feel comfortable and secure, yet it was a pretty monstrous home to live in, with four hundred staff and anything up to seven hundred guests at any one time.

Her own suite somehow seemed bigger than when she had

first seen it with Sally. The bicycle had taken up more space than one would have guessed, and then she had been careful not to bring in too much clutter. Her clothes were neatly put away in the fitted drawers and cupboards and, apart from adding a few books, two oil paintings and several bright cushions, the sitting room was as she had found it. The colour scheme was pleasant, considering the fittings were modern; grey tones with brown and white, nothing that jarred, and she had to admit that for the first time in her life she actually enjoyed putting her feet up to watch afternoon television for the one hour off she allowed herself. Between three and four was always a dead time, before the onslaught of the evening activities, and she soon learned to make the most of it.

So there she was, New Year's Eve, three months into the job and a success. In this business, compliments weren't handed out on a plate, but she had had her share from the people who mattered, to the point that she actually wondered whether there was something about her which she hadn't quite figured out but which was apparently irresistible to others. She had developed a sharpness of wit and an ability to make people laugh and feel at ease, she had smoothed over five really big problems and several smaller ones. She had enabled Vivien to take a five-day vacation with her family away from it all after a hectic Christmas week. Tonight, at the Grand New Year's Eve Gala Ball, which she had suggested and organized, she had been invited to the President's table with all the company directors and managers.

Natalie had not expected this, had not planned it at all. Her idea had been to stay in the wings and just make sure that everything ran smoothly, but Martineau had told her that Krieselman wanted her to be at the main table, and then she had received a letter from the man himself, the big white chief, requesting her to seat herself on his left, with Martineau's wife on his right as his honoured guest.

Naturally she had bought herself another dress, expensive, very expensive, but as a month back she had decided that the hotel was going to be her way of life, spending some of her well-earned money making it even more enjoyable was fully justified. Appearances in her job were all important anyway and, realizing from a survey in one of the trade magazines that she was probably one of the youngest PR people in the business to hold such a position, this had given her a great deal of confidence.

She had slept with one or two people to help her on her way up, or out of a jam, and though she had guiltily considered that it might be a form of prostitution she had decided that it was not, because she had enjoyed both occasions and done the choosing.

Grant, admittedly, had made her wonder whether she'd lost her self respect, but he had been an experience, not to be repeated, but an experience. He was a rough man, had been rough from the word go, boorish, crude, nearly violent, but with him she had done things she had never done before because she had thought young ladies shouldn't. It had been surprisingly enjoyable. All the blazing lights in the small bathroom with him behind her was something she would not easily forget, in fact she remembered it every time she had a bath, and she still got a tingle of pleasure at the memory. She had not been cornered into going to bed with him, or rather being humped as he would probably have said. She had just led him to a point where he had had to make the suggestion and she had accepted on her terms. After that he had waited patiently for his assistant to be moved to a different hotel and then one of his own choosing to be engaged, but the brief affair had somehow done her some good because it had soon got about that she was a woman who could take care of herself, and when the rumour spread that she had been had by the ginger-haired Scots engineer, she instantly seemed to gain the respect of the gay hierarchy which seemed to include half the hotel staff.

Martineau had not been one of her lovers, though it had got close enough at times. That one she didn't fancy, and she would lose his respect if she gave in. But a friend of his had caught her attention for more than one night. Three nights to be precise – a Dane who had drunk vast quantities without it apparently affecting him, and a man who could apparently be of use to Martineau if he was well entertained.

He had, for some reason, decided that the PR girl with

short blonde hair and the wicked smile was what he wanted, so Martineau had gone round in circles and nearly got down on his knees to ask her to be 'kind'.

It had paid off handsomely.

The Dane had been unprecedently generous and given her a gold bracelet, and Martineau had somehow managed to put up her salary, no skin off his wallet, but a handsome reward indeed.

Now it was company president night and as she was expected to make the party go with a swing, she would do so, first, by oiling her own little brain at the Panorama Bar with a drink or two, then checking up that all the seat placings were right in the Monarch Ballroom, and that the band would know what to play when, and that the chefs and commis and waiters were all aware of who was who without kow-towing too much.

'Mr Victor Krieselman,' she would tell them, 'likes to think he comes incognito, but God help anyone who fails to recognize him.'

She looked at herself once more in the mirror, the kiss curl in the centre of her forehead was unusual, but amusing, as the girl in the hair salon downstairs had said. Her make-up was not too over the top, the shoes OK, everything else all-stations-go. She left her suite with her tiny gold chain-mail handbag, and took the lift to the top floor.

She always entered the Panorama Bar with a little fear and trepidation since she had seen the 'hotel ghost'. She had talked about it to several people, partly to laugh it off and partly to find out if anyone else had seen it, but nobody had, indeed the lady cleaner whom Sally had mentioned refused to talk about it and the room service manager had laughed off the suggestion that he had ever seen an apparition.

She deliberately sat down on the very seat the old man had sat on and asked Steve for a champagne cocktail.

Drinks were free, food was free, bed and breakfast and even toothpaste was free. In the last three months she had actually stashed away nearly all her salary, had gone into the black for the first time in four years and at this rate would be able to buy herself a little car and all the other perks that went with having money!

Martineau came up unexpectedly, wearing his dinner jacket, lace fronted shirt, and velvet bow tie, looking immaculate if a little weary.

'I hate New Years,' he said, 'nearly as much as I hate Christmases.'

'What can I offer you?' she asked. It was a silly routine to go through, but it gave the impression in front of junior staff that everyone paid for the drinks they actually consumed. What happened was that her charge sheet went straight from the accountant to Martineau who signed it away as essential expenses. Apart from which it was well known that she did not drink that much.

How could she? A clear head was vital at all times, and she was the last person to want to become an alcoholic, which was one of the major hazards of the profession.

'Same as you,' he said. 'I've just been looking at the seating plan for our table. You've got Robert Clariss sitting next to you, have you ever met him?'

'No.'

Robert Clariss was a special guest of the Krieselmans' and manager of the Beaumont Plaza in Paris.

'I think he may try to wrestle you away from me,' Martineau whispered in her ear.

An offer of a Paris PR job?

'My French wouldn't be up to it,' she said modestly.

'It would after a while, and it's not a French hotel. They want to improve the class of international jet setters staying there and need an imaginative PR. I've sung your praises so much that I may have unwittingly helped to lose you.'

'I'm flattered.'

'You know, of course, that in-fighting within the company is encouraged. We, of the managerial club, have to compete with each other, and stealing staff is looked upon as fair game.'

'You mean if he offers me more you may have to put up my salary again?'

'I'm quite ready to do that.'

'I think it's a bit too early for me to leave here.'

'I think so too. But he could make you an offer you can't

refuse. Besides which, he is an appealing man himself.'

'So I had better watch myself?'

'I'll watch yourself. You just watch *out*.'

As it turned out, what she liked best about Robert Clariss was that he did not once attempt to make a cheap pass at her during the whole evening, nor did he allude to her being unpartnered, or himself being alone, or even hint that he was a manager of a more important hotel. The dinner, he made it clear, the whole evening, was to be enjoyed.

Victor Krieselman and his wife behaved remarkably well for people with so much power, and all the staff did their jobs perfectly.

When she went to bed, at about four in the morning, she was truly satisfied with her efforts. All had gone well: the singing of Auld Lang Syne had been rowdy but fun, the champagne had flowed, and nobody had misbehaved, which was extraordinary because five hundred or so people had drunk an awful lot.

She woke up the next day wondering whether the coming year could be as successful as this last one, and it seemed to her that if she could manage to keep things going as she had up to now, she could count herself lucky.

She was about to swing her feet round to the floor and get up, when the phone rang.

It was Robert Clariss.

'We met last night, we sat next to each other,' he said, with a laugh in his voice.

'I do remember.'

'Are you doing anything for lunch today?'

'No,' she answered, 'it's about the one day in the year that I'm not. Nobody dares make any appointments. Besides which it happens to be Sunday.'

'I would like you to have lunch with me, preferably away from your Palace. Could you join me in the bar of the Ritz Hotel, from whence I shall take you to a place of my own choosing?'

They agreed a time and she had a long pleasant bath feeling that the New Year might turn out OK.

Martineau had been right then; Robert Clariss was head

hunting. How was she to play the game? She liked it here, didn't really want to move, but if she was going to be a career girl then good opportunities should come before comfort.

She'd just have to see what was proposed.

Paris was certainly a carrot.

She dressed in one of her elegant suits, went down to reception where two of the staff had failed to turn up, and asked the doorman to get her a taxi.

The Ritz was less crowded than it would be on a normal Sunday: most customers were talking in low voices about their hangovers and their previous night's parties, and a few lonely people looked even lonelier. It happened in London, some people just didn't have friends.

Robert Clariss was waiting for her, they had a drink over which they too discussed the previous evening's highlights. Then they drove out to the country in a hired car – large, comfortable, not to impress but simply because it was convenient and on expenses.

He talked about Paris and his work, the hotel he ran, then switched to his marriage, the one that had not worked out, and asked her about herself.

They went up the Thames Valley to Marlow, to the Compleat Angler where they had a window seat overlooking the river. It was delightful and she appreciated the change of environment.

'Have you any idea why I've invited you on this clandestine lunch?' he asked.

'It could be one of two things,' she answered, cutting delicately through her smoked salmon.

'Name them.'

'No. It might prove presumptuous of me, specially if I'm wrong.'

'Be brave, make a mistake or two.'

'You either want to know some state secret regarding the running of the Palace Plaza, or you want me to go to bed with you,' she said, hoping she was playing her cards carefully.

'Right on the second count.'

'What's the first reason then?'

'I want you to join me in New York. I've been given the

Park Avenue Palace.'

She had seen it happening in films and she had never thought it realistic or likely, but now she actually choked. She drank some water quickly, he came round to pat her on the back, but, unlike the movies, she did not get over it quickly but went puce in the face and had to go to the ladies' powder room to recover her composure.

Paris with all its beauty had had its appeal at the back of her mind, but New York was something else. New York she loved! It was the new world, it was everything that she found exciting and stimulating and the Park Avenue was a glorious, old-fashioned hotel which, like so much of New York, was seeped in the 1930s art nouveau atmosphere she found so stylish.

Martineau would have to come up with something astounding to beat that one.

She returned to the table and ate her smoked salmon and drank down her glass of white wine before opening up the conversation again.

'Why me?'

'I don't have to sing your praises and you don't have to fish for compliments. In three months you've proved that you're exceptionally good at your job. I'm starting in New York at the end of February and I'd like to start with you on my team. I can arrange everything as far as contracts with Martineau are concerned, it's simply up to you.'

'Same conditions of living?'

'The same, and an equivalent salary.'

'How long do I have to think about it?'

'Not long. I'm flying to New York on Tuesday to present all my proposals. I'd like to know before I go.'

It occurred to her that she might not like the hotel, its environment, that she might be wrong about living in Manhattan.

'Permits? Work permits, all that?'

'We have ways.'

The wine was just beginning to take effect, she was feeling whoozy and knew the danger signs. Though it might be her day off, this was business like never before and she had to be cautious.

'What about the other reason?' she said, suddenly knowing that she had to attack the subject now or never. 'Don't you think that a . . . relationship . . . could be awkward, in business terms?'

'I'm not a jealous man.'

'I might be a jealous woman.'

'I don't think so. I think you know which side your bread is buttered. If you're going to work for me it's always going to be an issue between us. So I'd like that to be dealt with first.'

It was a stunningly blunt approach.

He was very sure of himself, was Mr Clariss. He was so sure of himself that he was daring her to turn him down, but of course he was right, it would always be between them, and could become unbearable. If she turned out to like him, well fine. If she didn't . . . but she did like him, or their conversation wouldn't have got this far and she wouldn't have accepted his lunch invitation in the first place.

'OK,' she said, with light-hearted enthusiasm. 'Where and when?'

'Now. Your place or mine?'

'The hotel? People will talk.'

'I expect they're talking already.'

He drove back slowly.

She had drunk a brandy, which had been a mistake and after last night she felt sleepy, and closed her eyes. When she opened them they were driving down Gloucester Road and then entering the hotel garage.

'We can take the lift straight up to the seventeenth floor, unless you need to go to your room first,' he said.

So cautious these men, so scared of getting maidens pregnant.

They stepped into the lift. Room 1711 was one of the bridal suites overlooking the park. It was four o'clock, one of those grey winter's days turning to dusk, always a little sad and lonesome. She was pleased she was with him.

'What can I offer you?' he asked.

'Tea?'

It was hours past tea time, but she ordered it anyway.

They sat opposite each other on respective sofas. They had not touched much, certainly not kissed.

'You might not like me,' she said.

'I might not. Let's hope I don't, then I'll be able to be cruel and unkind and shout at you which will make my job a lot easier.'

She knew the girl who brought the tea in, looking very tired. She was sleeping with Steve, the Panorama barman.

She told Robert, who was amused.

'You see, you're so knowledgeable on all levels. Just what a hotel PR should be. A detective and a gossip as well as a diplomat. You're very good.'

'Is anyone else likely to come in?' she asked.

'No.'

'Then if you don't mind I'll kick off my shoes,' which she did, tucking her feet under her legs and snuggling down in the sofa.

'When are you due back on duty?' Robert asked.

'Tomorrow, nine o'clock.'

'We have all night.'

'It should be enough.'

She realized that since Felix had left her she had put up no defences at all against men's advances. She had even thought of seeing a psychiatrist, but then she had decided that there was no point since she knew exactly what the problem was. She liked sex. To deny herself something which was absolutely natural would be stupid, and she had dropped all pretences that sex was only supposed to happen within a relationship.

She did not exactly collect men but she went to bed without fuss when the occasion presented itself, never expecting anything from it but physical pleasure and perhaps a useful friendship. Useful was the key word. She never missed out on a useful contact, which was perhaps why she had got so far.

Now, as she sat sipping the champagne he had ordered after they had finished the tea, watching Robert Clariss watching her, she was pleased that it was her female prerogative to do nothing.

He was, it seemed, getting excited at the prospect of what he had set up. She judged him in advance, decided that he would be meticulous, clinical, a selfish lover, that he might demand something a little out of the ordinary, and that he would not think she would expect anything in return. She would have to pay, in fact, for the so-called gift, the New York offer, by being a victim of his lust. And that thought quite excited her. To be told what to do and very nearly dislike what had to be done would have its merits if he was commanding enough. Maybe she was a masochist. It would certainly be a disappointment if he turned out to be a weak man who expected the woman to take the initiative. He couldn't though. He could not have got where he was without being an imposer.

'Would you like another bottle?' he asked, placing his empty glass on the table close to him.

'No thank you.'

'You may need it.'

She raised her eyebrows.

'Will you do exactly as I ask you?'

'Of course.'

'Then when you've finished your champagne I would like you to undress.'

Delightful. She was already beginning to feel frightened.

'In here?' she asked.

'In here.'

It was dark outside, but the curtains were still open. She would have to make it as erotic as possible.

She finished her champagne and put her glass down, swung her legs to the floor together, and put her arms down by her side, her hands holding onto the edge of the sofa, looking at him. Maybe he was testing her strength of character. It wasn't that easy taking one's clothes off in front of a critical male without losing one's nerve. She would have to do it calmly, elegantly. Prostitutes were asked to do this sort of thing every day, maybe twice or three times an evening. There was absolutely no reason why she shouldn't cope.

She started by undoing the buttons of her blouse. She undid them all, opening her jacket wider to do so. She then stood up, took off her jacket, undid the zip of her skirt and let it drop to the floor. She was thankful that it was made of sufficiently silky material to slip off without getting stuck.

She was aware that the stockings she was wearing, reaching high up her thighs, were sexy – that was why she had worn them – so she kept them on till last, shaking off the blouse, then her bra and her slip to stand there feeling petite and vulnerable, her well proportioned body and her pert little breasts totally exposed.

She looked down at him and noticed that there was something stirring.

'Let's go to the bedroom,' he said, quickly getting up and leading the way. 'You can get into bed.'

It seemed he was pleased. She was glad to get in between the sheets, and now it was her turn to watch him.

He took off his clothes rapidly, shyly hiding himself as much as he could and even getting in beside her still wearing his briefs.

Men were strange creatures.

He reached out for her and kissed her.

It was a disappointment.

Then he fumbled and moved about in the bed taking off his briefs and she felt him on her, long and hot, looked up at him to see that he had his eyes closed.

He wasn't very fond of himself, this man, he was not what she had expected or wanted, so she decided to take the initiative and got him to lie on his back. She got on top of him, watching him enjoying it all. New York! New York! she said under her breath, catching sight of herself in the mirror of the half opened cupboard. Had the interior decorators placed it there for this very reason?

Quite suddenly he opened his eyes and tried to sit up, staring at something behind her.

She didn't have to turn round for she could see what it was in the reflection.

It was a human shape with very little substance, white gossamer lengths of vapour with shadows for eyes and nostrils, a hole in the air for a mouth which smiled quite fearfully.

When she turned abruptly it was not there.

When she looked in the mirror again it had gone.

Inside her she felt Robert straighten painfully, and when she looked down at him she stared into the transfixed eyes of the dead.

CHAPTER THREE

Donald Southam lay on the double bed of Room 1712. The curtains were open, there were no lights on, it was one o'clock in the morning and he hadn't moved for three hours. He hadn't actually moved at all. Perhaps just his legs, crossing, recrossing them, perhaps a change of head angle, otherwise he had come straight in, taken off his jacket and shoes, stretched himself out on the bed, closed his eyes and had breathed in and out regularly trying to get things straight in his mind.

The room was going to cost him thirty pounds, if not more, – he hadn't bothered to check, hadn't asked the price. He had got out of the house, slammed the front door, had run senselessly into the night in the pouring rain, seen the bright lights of the hotel, the sheer luxury of it all, and had walked in. He had asked for a room, booked in, and kept the lowest profile ever from that moment.

His thoughts, when he had climbed up the wet marble steps, had been on suicide, not on the cost of the room. The height of the place had impressed him, he was fascinated and frightened by heights. The first time he had tried to take his life with drugs he had failed so completely that it had turned out to be a nightmare of emotional blackmail for himself and his family, which is why he had run away and married too quickly and was back where he had started – misunderstood.

He had been born to be a single person, a bachelor married to his art. That was very clear. No one else but another musician could possible sympathise with him. No one else but another creative artist. With grim determination to shake off his negative attitudes towards his work, he had let himself be sucked into the circle of much richer people whose interest in him had promised to be stimulating, but they had turned out to be even worse, not understanding at all what it meant to be composing music in the twentieth century. Luxury they had given him, a grand piano, a room of his own, everything that was needed for him to compose, but they had read the life of Tchaikovsky, read that Madame Nadezhda Von Meck had helped the great composer and had expected that their own daughter would play the same part. After two years, and no great ballet danced at Covent Garden, nor great concerto or symphony being heard at the Royal Festival Hall or on Radio Three, they had slowly and surely put on the pressure, perhaps without realizing it. 'Why don't you write for films? Why don't you write television themes? Why don't you write advertising jingles or pop music? You can make a lot of money that way.'

The independence he'd wanted was not financial, though probably it was what was needed. He wasn't sure. Certainly he knew that he could no longer write in that house because of the incessant interruptions now that his in-laws had moved back in from the country after the Christmas festivities.

'But you've got everything you want!' Cathy had pleaded.

'I've got everything but peace.'

She did not understand. None of them did. The simple interruption of thought when someone came into the room to ask him what he was doing because he was seemingly gazing out of the window was totally destructive. He had tried. God, he had tried to discipline himself, to compose between certain hours, arrange with her and her parents that he would write between nine and five with a break for lunch. But the break for lunch ruined the day. A gong was actually sounded by the maid, and loudly.

A gong!

In his head he'd had three violins intricately counterpointing.

'We could invite that successful conductor for dinner one evening, if it would help Donald,' had been the last suggestion. 'You know, the one who does the Promenade

Concerts. I'm sure father can arrange it.'

Of course 'father' couldn't arrange it. He had money, but no knowledge of what these people were about. Mention Glazunov or Mussorgsky or Hindemith and he'd ask whether they were running in the two-thirty at Epsom!

Why had he been born musical? Neither his parents were, nor his sisters. He had won a musical scholarship to a good school and the Royal College of Music, and from the moment he had gone there he should have thought of teaching, composing in his own spare time. Instead he had got married to money, thus severing any ties he had with his own parents because they felt inferior to his new family.

An impossible situation.

So now he was lying on the seventeenth floor of this new hotel which he had seen rise up, changing the skyline he could see from his very own window.

He had taken so many walks in Hyde Park, watching it go up, round and round the Round Pond, with music in his head. He had tried, by God, to understand what went on in other people's ears. He had listened to pop music, to disco music, walking with his Sony Walkman plugged in. It had made him hate ducks and squirrels and toy sailing boats for ever. Then he had looked south at the Albert Hall and this huge new edifice with its black glass and copper façia rising. He had watched the cranes, the outside lifts going up and down. He had composed music to it. He had done that much. The lifts. *The Elevators*, a short composition for piano and flute by Donald Southam. Then off she'd gone, mother-in-law, to EMI and the BBC with a tape, suggesting they should make a record. They would if they ever cut a miscellany of twentieth-century British composers. They knew his work, had heard of him, but . . . but . . . but . . .

'Mother and Father are coming back, they'll be here till the summer holidays, they'll be here for the season.'

Their arrival in the middle of his cantata had been too much and he had blown up.

Rightly he had been accused of not being grateful, and once again the little pin-pricks, the little accusations had darted across the dinner table. 'Have you had any success with your music lately, Donald? Why don't you become a concert pianist? I see James Galway has a programme of his own, now there's a clever man, talented and capable of making money.'

'If you don't like living with us then you should go,' Cathy had said. So he had gone. Picked up his jacket up and left the house and not really come down to earth till he had realized how wet he was. Then he'd been grateful for having had the sense to take his wallet, with the credit cards, American Express, courtesy of his wife's family of course. Well, he could run up a steep bill on that for a month or two before they got worried and sent in the heavies. Cathy's father would pay eventually anyway.

His mouth felt dry and he realized he was thirsty.

He had written a funeral march which one publisher had bought. They were not sure when they would use it, but had hinted that they might try to sell it for a state occasion. Why didn't he write something more cheerful? Like a wedding march? So he had, and a few days later the Royal Engagement had been announced and the market had been flooded with wedding marches. Writing commercially was hopeless.

He switched on the light and got up to go to the bathroom. Everything so incredibly clean. The glass was new, engraved with a Palace Plaza coat of arms. He turned on the lovely shiny tap, let it run for a while then filled the glass up with crystal clear water and drank.

It was beautiful.

He moved to the bedroom window and looked out. He was looking North East; he could see the red light of the Post Office tower, the orange glow of Marble Arch, the spike of the Albert Memorial above the trees and the dome of the hall itself.

Well, at least he had played there several times, in an orchestra admittedly. The flute.

He checked his watch – two in the morning. He had to get out and have something to eat. He didn't want to pick up the phone, felt too shy for that, but would have a wander around the silent hotel to see if there was someone about who could help him.

He put on his shoes and his jacket and left the room with the key. As he turned to go down the corridor he saw this very strange procession coming out of the next door room.

First came a man in a charcoal grey suit, with a white shirt and green tie; then a girl, youngish, certainly attractive, with short cut blonde hair, looking rather upset, rather concerned; then two men pulling out a trolley on which there was a long metal box.

He didn't know for sure but he guessed that the box contained a dead person. That is how they dealt with the deceased in hotels and apartment blocks. They put the corpses in a discreet metal box and got them out of sight as quickly as possible.

The girl looked at him, smiled bravely and followed the trolley, then she stopped and said something to the man in the grey suit and came back towards him.

'You look lost. Can I help you? I'm staff.'

'I was wondering if I could get something to eat.'

She thought for a moment, checked her watch, then quite sweetly said, 'Most of the services are closed at this time of night, but you could join me upstairs for a snack. I need one myself.'

They had reached the lift doors and she touched the square electronic call button.

She took him up to the top floor, the Panorama Bar and Restaurant where there was a band playing a tango. A party of people were at a far table, laughing, drinking, and from the look she exchanged with the head waiter it was clear that he feared the party would keep him up till morning.

'You keep long hours,' Donald suggested.

'The band normally stops at one o'clock, unless it's a special party and they're requested to play on. But they get double time for doing so.'

They sat down at a discreet corner table behind a column where they could not be seen by others.

"The kitchens are actually closed but we can have a cold salad, and whatever you want to drink.'

'I leave it to you,' he said.

She got up and disappeared through the service doors.

It was fate, then. An angel had been sent to save his life. He certainly no longer had any intention of killing himself. Not that he had thought of doing so that seriously. He liked her short cut hair and the funny curl on her forehead.

'What exactly do you do?' he asked, when she came back and sat down opposite him.

'Assistant PR. I look after the welfare of the guests,' she said.

'You had an unpleasant evening it seems.'

'Yes. Someone died in the room next to yours, as you saw.'

'As I guessed.'

'I hope you won't mention it to anyone else. It can upset some people.'

'I don't know anyone else here,' he said.

The head waiter came dancing up to them, all smiles, and placed a large platter of fresh salmon on the table and another of York ham and various other cold meats, then an ice bucket with an open bottle of champagne.

For a moment he thought he might have to make noises about the cost, but the girl was quick in sensing his discomfort and put him immediately at ease.

'Who's our benefactor?' she asked, as the head waiter filled their glasses.

'Table twenty-six again.'

'To Mr twenty-six!' she said, raising her glass.

'Does this happen often?'

'No, but we have a South American couple staying here at the moment who come up every night, order a bottle of champagne which they never finish, so we do. It's silly to waste it.'

He hadn't expected this.

Barely two hours ago he was contemplating death, now he was drinking champagne to the perfectly acceptable beat of a waltz. Noel Coward, which he liked, the band was playing a selection from *Bitter Sweet.* Perhaps he should write a musical?

'Are you from far away?' she asked.

'No. I live round the corner, in Kensington Terrace Square.'

'Very pretty,' she said, curious, obviously, but in no way prying.

'My wife's house. Her family's. I'm a composer by trade, a musician, and as such not very well off, but I married into money, which hasn't worked.'

'I'm sorry.'

'My wife doesn't understand me,' he said jokingly.

'Who does?' she asked, leaning over the table and looking into his eyes teasingly.

'I've never asked myself that question. Perhaps no one?'

She screwed up her nose at him, amused. He was used to that sort of reaction. Women liked teasing him, it had something to do with his permanent look of perplexity. As a little boy he had been teased, and he was still a little boy, when it suited him.

'What sort of music do you compose?' she asked.

'Does Shoenberg mean anything to you?'

'Not much.'

'Bela Bartok?'

'Discords to the untrained ear, you mean?'

'Yes.'

'Classical then. Modern, but for Radio Three?'

'Exactly.'

'I doubt whether I can be sympathetic. Do you play an instrument, or is that a stupid question? I know nothing about composing.'

'I play most instruments, but the piano is my first love, then the flute.'

The band stopped and started packing up, the crowd in the corner clapped politely and the head waiter sailed past, opening his eyes wide and waving the bill in way of celebrating the end of his day.

'We'll have to leave soon, I'm afraid,' she said.

'Didn't you want to go to bed?' he asked.

She raised an eyebrow.

He had meant it perfectly innocently but understood what she might have thought. She lived in such a different world to his!

'I'm not a bit tired,' she quickly admitted, again putting

him at ease, 'If it's stopped raining we could go for a walk.'

It was a marvellous idea, and just what he felt like doing.

They walked along the wide pavement by the Park towards Knightsbridge, the occasional taxi cruising past, the occasional night bus, and late walkers like themselves.

'What are you going to do about your family?' she asked.

'I have no idea. Right now I want to go to sleep and wake up so that it'll be another day.'

He started telling her all that had been in his mind, trying to explain the frustrations he felt because of imposed restraints which was the price he had to pay for supposed freedom. It was Catch 22.

'I know the feeling.'

'You had a bad time tonight?' he asked again, wanting to bring her out, wanting to be just as sympathetic to her problems.

'He was a youngish man, late forties, and I happened to be with him.'

'I'm sorry.'

They walked on silently. He wasn't sure what else to say, but she broke the silence.

'It was such a shock.'

'Had you known each other a long time?'

It was clear that she wanted to talk, needed to, and as he was a stranger in the night whom she might never see again, it was probably safe. That's how he felt about it anyway.

'He was the manager of another hotel who had offered me a better job, but I didn't think I'd get it, or rather that my chances of getting it would be reduced unless I slept with him.'

'Things like that really go on? Such pressure?'

'They go on but shouldn't be misinterpreted. It was my choice entirely. PR girls do tend to get a bad reputation but only because they mix with so many more people than most and have so many more opportunities to enjoy themselves. Like air hostesses. They have a reputation for enjoying sex. Sex is enjoyable, after all.'

She looked down at the pavement. He had to admit that she was right. It played a certain part in the mood of his music, sex, and perhaps, if he would only admit it, it was an important aspect in his marriage which had vanished along with all the other things he had so enthusiastically embraced on first becoming involved with his new family.

'What you should do,' she said, 'is go back home now. You look suitably worn out and repentant. You're not going to give up your wife and a whole way of life because of an argument concerning your in-laws' attitudes. You should go home and tell her you had something creative going on in your head which you had to sort out. Does she know what you're working on?'

'No. Not really.' There was so much to explain.

'Well then, why not tell her what she wants to hear, what they want to hear, that you are writing something commercial?'

'But that would be deceiving her.'

'Walking with a strange girl near the Park at night after having dinner with her is much more of a deception.'

At the corner of the street she kissed him very briefly on both cheeks and wished him good night and good luck.

'What about my room? The bill?' he asked.

'You said you hadn't even got into bed.'

'I used the glass in the bathroom.'

'I think that can be overlooked.'

As he walked away he realized he did not even know her surname and that she was the first person in years who had been really kind to him, and he decided that first thing in the morning he would send her some flowers.

She had certainly made him feel that life had other dimensions than those within which he was at present living.

Natalie didn't sleep at all.

She lay on her bed and watched dawn break over the London sky hoping she would doze off, but every time she did the fearful image of Robert's face, and his expression of sheer horror, loomed up, haunting her semi-consciousness.

She didn't want to admit it, didn't want to think of the hideous experience, but she had seen a ghost and he had seen a ghost, and it had killed him.

Who would believe it?

There would be an enquiry of course. His wife, his children would get involved, the fact that she had been with him when he died would come out and she would lose her job.

At seven o'clock she fell asleep, only to be woken up by room service with her morning coffee a few minutes later.

Why hadn't she gone to bed? the girl asked. Why hadn't she undressed? What had she been doing? Did she know that a Mr Clariss had died in Room 1711?

After the coffee she had a shower. Today, with luck, there would be nothing too complicated to add to the inevitable enquiries. She dressed casually, put on a little make up.

By a quarter past eight she was at her desk, opening the morning mail, and the expected call came through punctually at nine. It was Martineau, asking her to come to his office.

'Tell all,' he said.

She told all, without mentioning what she had seen in the mirror, what she really thought had killed him. Martineau and his superiors would hardly accept a ghost story as an excuse for what they would obviously consider to have been an over-zealous bout of love-making.

'Who knew you were with him?' he asked.

'Derek Edgars and two security men.'

'No one else?'

'Room service maybe. We had tea at four o'clock.'

'Then there should be no problem. We can contain it. It's between you, me and Edgars, and will remain that way for ever. In exchange for which discretion I must ask you to inform his family what happened.'

'That's horrible!'

'It's called poetic justice.'

She wanted to question whether he had the right to set himself up as a judge, but decided it would be wrong to argue. Instead she went to her suite from where she asked for Robert's Paris home number on the phone and, in the peace of her own environment, got through to Mrs Clariss.

The voice was hard, metallic, rather indifferent.

'Mrs Clariss?'

'Speaking.'

'My name is Natalie Weir, I am Mr Martineau's assistant at the London Palace Plaza . . .'

'Yes? What can I do for you? I know Mr Martineau well.'

Was there as much to that sentence as she imagined?

'I have some extremely bad news for you.'

Was that the way to present it? How did you announce a death?

'Something has happened to David?'

David? David Martineau? The give away use of the Christian name! The concern for the wrong man. It made it easier.

'No . . . to your husband.'

'Goodness . . . what?'

'He had a heart attack . . .'

'Oh my God!'

'I'm afraid he died this morning, at about one o'clock.'

Was there a formula, a better way of saying it? There was a terrible silence at the other end of the line and she waited a while, then enquired if she was all right.

'Yes. I'm still here. What on earth happened?'

'He was found when he failed to answer the alarm call. We would suggest an autopsy . . .'

'I'll ring David . . . Mr Martineau.'

Oh, that deceit should dwell in such a gorgeous palace!

Somehow she felt better, but needed to talk to someone, preferably over a stiff drink.

She went along to her office and found Vivien waiting for her.

'Sit down sweetie, close the door.'

She closed the door, sat down opposite her.

'Do you want the day off?'

'Frankly, I don't know. Maybe I should go and have a rest, on the other hand I want to be kept busy so I don't have to think of what happened.'

'Did he offer you the New York job?'

'Yes. You knew about it?'

'I'd heard it was going. Did you accept?'

'I didn't have the chance.'

'Well, don't if it comes up again, because I'm putting you up for promotion here. And this, in fact is worth more.'

'How do you mean?'

'New York would only have been assisting, which means carrying the can for the Americans. Promotion here means my job.'

'What?'

'I wasn't going to tell you till the end of the month but as you deserve some good news, self is leaving.'

'Does Martineau know?'

'Oh yes. And you're up for the post. Now you'll get it because you've behaved in an exemplary way, and you've joined the club.'

'How do you mean?'

'The staff call it Randies Anonymous.'

'I'm not sure I like that.'

"Gossip can be lethal, so just take my advice and be even more discreet. Pity you haven't got a boyfriend as a cover.'

'Maybe I have. Does the fact that he's married matter?'

'Here? You must be joking! Just flaunt him around. It confuses people and affairs are best managed under a blanket of confusion.'

Instead of going back to her suite to have a rest, Natalie went up to Room 1711, getting the pass key from Room Service, and locked herself in.

She went from the living room to the bedroom to the bathroom, went back to sit down on the sofa where she had sat opposite Robert, then went to lie down on the bed, after opening the cupboard door so that she could see herself in the mirror. Then she faced the wall.

Her imagination got the better of her and she began to feel frightened. On hearing a noise she turned round ready to see the reflection of something quite terrible. The room was quite empty and the noise continued, however, something in the pipes, or the wind against the windows, nothing that could not be explained.

Had she imagined it all in the heat of the extraordinary moment, had it been a premonition, or his spirit leaving him at the moment of death?

She had seen the old man in the Panorama Bar. Sally had seen the old man.

She went round the suite again, opened all the cupboards, looked behind the curtains and under the bed, half to make sure that all Robert Clariss's belongings had been taken out, half to satisfy herself that there wasn't some diabolical machine which some practical joker might have planted.

She so wanted to find a realistic explanation!

She left and went down to her own room, where she found a large bouquet of flowers on the coffee table with a card.

It read: 'Thank you for doing more for me last night than you will ever realize. If I may I will call you soon. Love. Donald.'

Was he a man who used the last word at random, or was it perhaps a little bit meant?

She smelt the roses and carnations. They were beautifully arranged. They hadn't come from the florist downstairs; he had bothered to go further afield, which was nice. Having recently learned all the intricacies of the hotel trade, would she now have to swot up on music?

She would. Beethoven! Chopin! Here I come!

She got undressed, feeling much more relaxed and deciding she'd try to get some sleep. Instead of sleep she started listing the classical composers she knew in alphabetical order. Forget the As for a start . . . B for Beethoven and Bartok, whom he had mentioned, C for Chopin, D for Debussy or Delius. Not bad so far. E for Elgar . . . F . . . G . . . H . . . If he sat down and played her something on the piano she would never be able to tell what he was playing. M for Mozart. W for Wagner . . . Her lids felt heavy and she started to doze off, but in her exhaustion the dreadful memory returned; Robert's eyes, closed, then opening in startled terror.

She sat up.

She remembered thinking that perhaps he had had an operation and that he had strained a muscle, or a stitch had snapped. It had seemed too physical. Then she realized he was in shock and staring at the presence behind her.

And it had been a female presence.

Strange. Why did she feel that the room had been invaded by something feminine?

All the time, since it had happened, deep down she had felt it was a woman. The apparition in the Panorama Bar had definitely been an old man.

But this had been an old woman. Would she be able to talk about it to Donald? He might be more receptive to such fantasies than others.

She lay down again and this time went to sleep, to be woken up by the phone ringing at five. It was Tania checking that she was all right. She apologized for disturbing her but asked whether she'd remembered that Carmel Dreihardt's PRO was arriving at six for the first meeting to discuss publicity proposals.

Three days later something quite extraordinary occurred. It was frightening and very nearly impossible to explain.

She was in her office checking through the February bookings when the head waiter from the Sovereign Suite came rushing in, panting, white, asking if she would come along, straight away.

'What on earth's happened?'

'You wouldn't believe me if I told you. Best see it for yourself.'

As she followed him quickly down the corridor, walking as casually as possible so as not to arouse the suspicions of the hotel guests, she remembered that there was a children's birthday party in the Sovereign and that probably some dreadful little boy had done something fearful in the presence of elderly ladies.

But it was not that. It was not that at all.

Some forty children and parents who had been sitting down to tea were grouped silently by the door staring in disbelief at the long table they had left in a hurry.

Down its centre, stuck firmly through the white tablecloth into the wood, were some twenty sharply pointed silver butter knives, not quite in a straight line, humming as they quivered inexplicably.

CHAPTER FOUR

'Who did that?' Natalie asked.

'No one. It just happened,' the head waiter said nervously. 'As the guests sat down and were about to be served sandwiches, the knives leapt up of their own accord and stuck themselves in the table.'

She was about to remark that it was impossible, about to tell him that he was mad, but checked herself.

For some terrible reason she believed him.

Slowly, watched by all those present, she stepped forward and pulled one of the knives out. It had been embedded so deeply in the table that it took some strength and effort.

She clutched it like a dagger and stuck it in the table again, but to make it stand up she found she had to use a great deal of force because the wood was very hard.

She turned to look at the guests, smiled and found she had an explanation for the phenomenon. 'I'm very sorry about this. It is a most unusual occurrence, but it has happened before.' She took a deep breath and mentally wished herself luck.

'When they were building this hotel,' she explained with surprising confidence, 'the construction company used a new steel composition for their structural girders. When they laid the electric cables down, the girders apparently became magnetised. By coincidence, this table has been positioned right along and above one of these magnetised girders, hence this quite entertaining result.'

Everyone instantly relaxed and mothers explained to the more curious children what had happened.

'The management apologizes for any discomfort caused, and if you would be kind enough to go to the Monarch Suite on the opposite side of the hallway, tea will be served promptly.'

There was relief in most of their eyes. One father started to argue with another as to the feasibility of the explanation, and when the crowd had left the room she found herself facing Martineau who very quietly, very discreetly clapped his hands.

'Where do you get your inspiration from, Natalie? It is nearly as inexplicable as the phenomenon itself.'

'I don't know.'

'Well, congratulations, and a hundred marks for imagination.'

'It doesn't explain it to us though, does it?'

'No.'

He looked at her for quite a while, then said, 'Tell me what you think, truly. I can guess but I want to hear it.'

'I think the place is haunted,' she said.

At which precise moment there was a fearful crash in the kitchen which adjoined the suite, followed by a scream.

Natalie clenched her fists and closed her eyes.

When she opened them again she saw Martineau doing the same. He was as tense as she was.

Then there were giggles and he puffed out his cheeks. Slowly, not rushing, both went to the kitchen to see what had happened.

On seeing them come in the staff straightened up and two of the younger waiters busied themselves picking up the remains of a tea tray that had been sent flying.

'What happened?' Martineau asked.

'The old story, sir,' the head waiter said, appearing from nowhere. 'The swing doors. One coming in one way, one going out.'

'They should be experienced enough by now . . .'

'Yes sir. But everyone is a little upset by the event, sir.'

'There's no reason to be,' Martineau commented. 'You heard Miss Weir's explanation. There is a magnetic field under certain floors. It always takes a while for faults to show themselves in new buildings,' with which he swept out, Natalie following.

The magnetic force theory made the rounds of the staff and the hotel guests and intrigued everyone. Providing the story didn't leak out to the Press, all would be well, and to make sure that it would not, Natalie asked reception to keep an eye out for any known reporters, or anyone else asking leading questions on the subject.

She had hardly got back to her desk when reception rang to tell her that a Mr Southam was there to see her. She said she would not be long, and to ask him to wait in the foyer.

That cheered her up.

She checked her looks in the mirror, then went down to find him rather well dressed with a dark red carnation in his button hole, sitting by the fountain.

He stood up immediately on seeing her.

'I was passing by,' he explained.

She looked at him warmly and they sat down next to each other. 'How are you, Donald?' she asked.

'Much better. I didn't want to come and see you until I had fully recovered my composure.'

'How is your wife and her family?'

'They've gone away for a whole two weeks.'

'Your doing, or theirs?'

'I told them I had been composing and actually sat down and played them some music they could understand. It worked miracles. I apologized for being testy and tense, and explained how difficult I found it trying something new. It pleased them and they decided that the best thing was for them to leave me alone for a while till I had finished the "oeuvre"! Now there's even talk of us moving to the country so that I can have a room at the bottom of the garden, like Mahler, and work there without being disturbed.'

'Good news for you, bad news for me,' Natalie said.

He smiled and raised an eyebrow. 'I must ask why?'

'I won't see you very much.'

'On the contrary, you can come down as a guest as often as you like.'

'Will your wife approve?'

He smiled again, laughed even. 'I wasn't aware that our relationship had developed so fast. But I will be very pleased if it does.'

'So who is going to look after you for the next fifteen days?' she asked.

'Oh, I'll look after myself. I am capable. I am in fact quite a good cook. That's why I came to see you, to invite you to dinner.'

'Any special day?'

'Evening, I had hoped. As you are so busy I thought you might want to consult your diary.'

She went to reception and rang up Tania to ask her to look up what night she might be free. She wasn't for the next four nights, but on Sunday she was.

'Sunday?' she suggested.

'That's very far away.'

'Tea time tomorrow, or lunch the day after.'

'Tea tomorrow.'

The house was very attractive.

It was all white and had a little domed turret on one side overlooking Kensington Terrace Square. The front door led into a spacious black and white tiled entrance hall where Donald kissed her lightly on both cheeks under a quite magnificent chandelier.

'The house has been converted into two apartments,' he explained, 'ground floor is in-law territory, first floor is ours.'

He opened some double doors and showed her into a darkened drawing room, and when he opened the shutters she felt she had stepped back into the past. It was crowded with Victorian furniture which would have been more suited to a country house, and though some of the pieces were quite obviously valuable, none were shown off to great effect and it was rather a waste of an elegant room.

'They don't have much taste, I'm afraid. The house belonged to an uncle who bought it as an investment.'

He led her up the majestic stairs and once on the first floor the atmosphere changed completely. The floors were varnished pine, the rooms were bright white with large modern paintings. They contained remarkably little furniture but what there was was good. In the corner of the living room was a quite beautiful grand piano, stacked with sheet music and, apart from a low sofa, there was absolutely nothing else.

'My office,' he said.

He showed her a simply laid out kitchen with a minimum of clutter, a bedroom with a double bed, and the little turret room with nothing in it but a rocking chair.

'Wife's think-tank,' he said. 'Would you like tea now?'

'I'd love some.'

They went into the kitchen where he switched on a kettle.

'While I'm having my tea will you play me something of yours?' she asked.

'Maybe.'

He made the tea, and she leaned against the door watching him. He was not really handsome. His face was rather long, his hair sandy, curly, he had blue eyes, sad eyebrows, a generous mouth, but in general a pathetic look which appealed to her mother instinct, as it no doubt had to other women.

He opened three tins before he found the tea, and then wasn't quite sure what to do with it.

'Can I help?'

'No . . . no . . . I have to manage myself. Does one put a tea bag in a teapot or straight in a cup?'

'Why not straight in one of those mugs?'

He failed to find the tray, but asked her to carry in the tin of biscuits which seemed rather light. On opening it she found it half full of raisins. He apologized and was quite some time before returning with the right one, a new sealed tin from Harrods which he opened.

She settled down on the sofa and he sat down at the piano without being asked again, then to her astonishment launched into a pleasing classical arrangement of Beatle songs.

'I had no idea,' she said when he'd finished.

'But this is my own!' he said.

A series of grating discords followed which apparently sent him into another world, for he closed his eyes and didn't seem to be aware of her presence any more. He went on for quite some time to the point that she felt rather embarrassed.

He finished as suddenly as he had begun, closed the lid of the piano, turned to look at her and sat on his hands.

'You didn't like it?'

'I didn't understand it.'

'Honest anyway. A lot of people pretend they do.'

She didn't know how geniuses worked but felt that this one was possibly a little too comfortable. Everything was being done for him and he didn't realize it. There had to be a struggle surely? The series of discords meant nothing to her, she felt, because there was nothing behind them. They were musical scales cleverly composed, no doubt, and brilliantly interpreted perhaps, but they did not stir her and that maybe was because Donald was a little bit spoilt.

They talked about his music and about her background, her two hours of freedom soon went by and she left to return to work.

They met several times after that, more often at the hotel where they had coffee in her room or lunch in one of the restaurants whenever she could take time off. He wasn't particularly interested in what she did, he certainly wasn't interested in people and though she tried to be sympathetic to the problems he was having with his composing, his complaints about the domestic front became more and more banal. Now that his wife and family had gone the daily woman was causing him anxiety. She tried to explain, as gently as she could, that unless he lived totally alone he would never be able to have complete peace. The alternative was to go completely the other way for a while.

'You should mix with twentieth-century people. You're in an eighteenth-century job as it is, if you cut yourself off completely you'll never be able to communicate, verbally or through your music.

'How do I do that?'

'Get some work.'

'I can't do anything.'

'You can play the piano.'

'I'm not good enough. If I were I'd have given concerts years ago. I'm a composer.'

'I wasn't thinking of classical playing,' she said. 'Why don't you come and play here in the early evenings, from seven till eight, until the band starts, in the Panorama Restaurant. You're a member of the musicians union, aren't you?'

He was wide eyed. 'But what would they say?'

'Who?'

'The family.'

'Well, they'd probably admire you for trying something new. But if it worries you, they needn't know. I think you should try it for therapy.'

He thought for a long time, then said, 'If I do it, it'll be to be near you.'

It was the first thing she set up on taking over from Vivien – two weeks' trial for the new pianist, and she didn't even have to consult Martineau, just make sure the Panorama Bar made more money.

The same day that Donald started, she was busy with Carmel Dreihardt's arrival, which meant journalists in all corners of the hotel and the organization of a Press conference.

He wasn't coming incognito, but with a blare of trumpets to address ten thousand people at Wembley. Other evangelists had done it before him, but he had a new message of hope for the young. In fact it was the same old message proclaiming the love of God, but put in a different way. He had his followers who sat out in silent vigil in the park opposite the hotel twenty-four hours before his plane landed from the States and this all helped to get the Palace Plaza in the papers and on television screens as a backdrop. It promised to be a good newspaper story and, the week before, she had got an unexpected call from Felix begging her to get him a room on the same floor as Dreihardt's suite. For old time's sake she managed it by moving two or three expected guests around and she took him up to the Panorama Bar to see how Donald was coping with his first-night nerves.

Donald sat at the piano dressed, as she had suggested, in a

pale grey suit, white shirt, pink tie; neat, nothing extraordinary. He played to perfection, and after a very little while seemed very much at home. Pianists did, she presumed, once they were in front of a keyboard. He had a list in front of him of what he had rehearsed. He was happy, was pleased to see her, and she waved at him when she had to leave.

Two good deeds.

The joy of being in a position of power was that not only you, but your friends could benefit.

Carmel Dreihardt arrived on schedule at nine o'clock. The foyer was packed with cameramen.

He was a tall, white haired man, dressed all in royal blue, sporting large square spectacles, with a broad toothy smile which was switched off a little too suddenly when it wasn't needed. Rumour had it that he was a charlatan making a fortune out of the gullible, of course, and she was sure that Felix was out to find a chink in his armour. She had begged him to keep a low profile and certainly never to blame the hotel for allowing him to infiltrate a guest's privacy.

She got Felix the room right next to Dreihardt's and whether he was going to use bugs or not was hardly her affair. No one was aware that she knew him and he had been intelligent enough to sign in under another name.

So two days went peaceably by. Donald played, Felix behaved, Carmel Dreihardt made headlines denouncing all established religions in an apparently astounding speech at Wembley which all the papers quoted. Twenty thousand new converts were claimed, thirty thousand T-shirts with his face and emblem were sold, thirty thousand balloons were released with his face on them, the whole razamataz was co-ordinated like an epic film and on his last night a candlelit procession started from outside the hotel, moved slowly round the Park and back.

The evangelist had settled down in his suite on the fifteenth floor for the night, the Press had gone home and Natalie went up to the Panorama Restaurant to see how Donald was getting on as interlude pianist while the band were having their twenty-minute midnight break, a more

elegant innovation she had thought up to replace the musak usually piped through.

She was sitting at the bar, having ordered an iced Cointreau, when Donald, playing Mood Indigo quite suddenly stopped and stood up.

Following his gaze she saw a youngish woman with an elderly couple come into the restaurant and sit down at a table close to the band.

His action brought total silence into the room which jarred him into sitting down again and playing on, making a few mistakes, but playing on, staring in disbelief at the new guests.

Natalie guessed the trio were his wife and her parents and, concerned for Donald's state of nerves, she checked with the barman to know how much longer he would be playing. He'd hardly started, but fortunately Charlie, the band pianist, was just round the back chatting with one of the waiters.

She quickly went to find him and, explaining the situation, asked him if he could relieve Donald. Charlie, always ready to oblige, crossed the small dance floor, surprised Donald by sitting down next to him on the piano stool and first taking over the left hand then the right, so that only a few diners were made aware that the musician had changed.

Natalie met Donald round the back of the bar and took his hand. He was shaking uncontrollably.

'Your wife and parents-in-law, I presume?'

'How did they know? How could they have known I was working here?'

'Your cleaning woman?'

'How would she know?'

'Perhaps you told her, indirectly?'

'I never told her anything.'

'Practising Cole Porter instead of discords, your tune list written out on hotel paper left on the piano? A number of calls from me or the restaurant manager overheard?'

'I suppose so . . .'

'So you've been discovered, but they haven't come here

in anger. I think you're making a mountain out of a mole hill. It's you who doesn't want to be seen here. They don't mind you being in the limelight.'

'A bar pianist? You're joking!'

'I think it's a suitably decadent profession for the black sheep of a middle class aristocratic family.'

'I think they've had me followed and spied on.'

'Splendid.'

'It would involve you . . . a divorce . . .'

'No it wouldn't. We haven't slept together.'

For some reason it made him blush, and he tried to say something but it just wouldn't come out.

'What am I going to do?' he asked eventually. 'They'll be home. I mean . . . it's awful. I don't want to see them. I don't want to discuss . . .'

He was interrupted by a fearful scream, a hideous bellow, then panic stricken shrieks.

Natalie rushed into the restaurant to see people grouping round the piano, Donald's parents-in-law standing in the middle of it all holding their daughter.

Steve, the barman, was there, and Derek Edgars, making space, clearing people away. Then she saw, slumped over the piano, an unconscious Charlie.

She grabbed one of the younger waiters by the sleeve and shook him. He seemed to be rooted to the floor, his mouth wide open, his tray of plates precariously balanced on the flat of his hand.

'What happened?'

'She just got up and stabbed him.'

'What?'

Charlie was being carried out by Edgars and the head waiter. His shirt front was red with blood, his eyes open, staring, his face drained of colour.

She wasn't sure, but it seemed that his assailant was Donald's wife. She then noticed something quite terrible about the young woman.

As she was led across the dance floor by her parents, Natalie realized that her eyes were not seeing anything around her.

Donald's wife was blind.

She had attacked Charlie believing it was Donald playing.

It needed all her resourcefulness and diplomacy to handle this one, especially as from the corner of her eye she saw Felix, who had watched the whole scene from the bar, slink out.

First things first.

She got the parents and the girl out of the room, and had the restaurant manager take them down to Martineau's office. Then she begged Donald, however hard it was for him, to go back to the piano and play for a few minutes to give her time to calm everything down.

'It's like falling off a horse. If you don't get right back in the saddle now you'll become neurotic about the piano for ever.'

'I can't . . .' he pleaded.

'For me?' she begged.

And that worked, which, she said to herself, would need thinking about when she had time.

After that she went down to Felix's room and knocked loudly on the door.

He was ages coming to answer it, obviously because he was already on the phone to his paper.

He opened up and let her in.

'What did you tell them?' she asked.

'It was too good to miss, Natalie.'

'Please, what did you tell them?'

'Murder in new hotel. Blind woman stabs pianist. I mean, it's pure Agatha Christie.'

'Did you have to?'

'It's my job. And I've had absolutely no joy with Dreihardt, other than everyone else's bonanza stories.'

'It's my job to keep the reputation of the hotel clean and pretty,' she said.

'Your first murder. People will flock to stay here.'

'It's not a pub. People don't flock to sedate hotels where they pay a hundred pounds a night for thrills.'

'It's also the second death in two weeks,' Felix pointed out, too pleased with himself.

'Who told you about the first?'

‘Staff. I’m a journalist. I find things out.’

‘Did you mention me?’

‘No, why should I?’

‘No reason at all.’

She shouldn’t have asked. Oh God she shouldn’t have asked. Felix of all people! Too smart to outsmart.

‘No reason? Come on! You and the pianist?’ he said, snapping his fingers. ‘Grief! PIANIST’S BLIND WIFE FINDS OUT INFIDELITY WITH HOTEL PR.’

‘Not true. If you publish anything like that I’ll sue!’

‘And get damned and the sack. Sooner or later,’ he said quietly, ‘I knew I’d face the terrible problem of integrity. Job first or loyalty to friends?’

‘Once we were lovers,’ she reminded him.

‘Old friends,’ he corrected.

‘Felix,’ she said softly, trying to reason with him, ‘I got you this room next to Carmel Dreihardt. One good turn deserves another.’

‘Of course, my sweet, I’ll see that you survive. I haven’t filed the story yet, just reserved a headline, but you can make a lot of money if you play your cards right. My paper, for a start, will offer you a great deal of cash for the story. Who is the pianist, anyway, and how long have you known him?’

‘Not a word, Felix. You’ll not get a word on the subject from me.’

‘Pity,’ he said. ‘A lot of money.’

He crossed the room, sat down on the edge of the bed, picked up the phone, dialled a number and stared at her.

‘Felix, please.’

‘Job first, friends after.’

He was a bastard.

It would mean the end of her career. Any scandal would.

Then he gently, very gently put the phone down and stared just passed her with exactly the same expression in his eyes as Robert Clariss’s on the night of his death.

Slowly she turned round and saw something quite extraordinary.

There were five or six feet between herself and the door.

There was a cupboard to the right, a painting on the wall to the left below which was the suitcase stand and a chest of drawers.

In that area, an area of maybe five square feet, there was a presence.

It was dark, not like smoke, not like a cloud, not like a figure or anything else she had ever seen or even imagined, but a dark presence, as though a void had formed behind her, a black hole, and within it there was the feeling of amusement, of someone, something, laughing. Yet there was no sound, there was no actual face, there was no shape, nothing but a feeling.

Then it went.

When she turned round to look at Felix, he had fallen forward on his knees and was curled up on the floor, fists clenched tightly as though he had suffered an agonising blow.

Without stepping forward, let alone touching him, she knew he was dead.

And she also knew for certain that something quite dreadful was living in the hotel.

CHAPTER FIVE

He should, of course, have told her from the word go, but he knew that if he had he would have lost her sympathy. He had hoped to keep Cathy's blindness a secret, to have Natalie as an outside friend, round the corner, with whom he could have another life. He had not expected the terrible jealousy, the terrible misunderstanding and, in a way, he wished to God it had been him that had been attacked.

At least he had played the piano for more than ten minutes after the tragedy and helped to get the place back to normal. Everyone had been wonderful. Though several tables of guests had left, quite a number had stayed on, and newer people, unaware of what had happened, had come in. The head waiter had wiped the blood off the carpet just under the piano, and he had played a selection from *Guys and Dolls*, reading the sheet music, making quite a number of mistakes, till the band had come up.

He'd worried about having to play with them, but the guitarist doubled on the piano. He'd left, smiling meekly at everyone as they clapped politely, and had gone down to her office.

Time to think, time to reflect. What would she think of him? It was not that he had lied about Cathy, it was that he had just not mentioned her disability.

He hadn't married for love. He was fond of her, had enjoyed taking care of her, entertaining her, music was her whole life, but then it had gone all wrong because of her meddling parents. And now this fit of lunacy. Attacking a man with a knife thinking it was him!

Natalie eventually came in, went straight to a cupboard to bring out a bottle of brandy and pour them both out a good measure.

She was terribly pale and he felt more concerned for her than anyone else because she took her job so very seriously and all this would mean no end of problems for her.

She sat behind her desk in her swivel chair, went round full circle a couple of times then stopped to face him.

'Charlie's just died,' she said simply.

'Charlie's *dead*?'

'She stabbed him twice in the stomach and it was meant to be you.'

He breathed in slowly, exhaled slowly, took a good mouthful of brandy and swallowed it down.

'A journalist friend of mine called Felix also died. I happened to be in his room when it happened. That's three deaths in two weeks, all of them in the most extraordinary circumstances. It's going to give the hotel a bad name!' And she laughed at that, allowing the laugh to become so hysterical that he got up and grabbed hold of her across the desk and shook her by the shoulders.

She calmed down, gave him a look of thanks.

'It feels as though the place is haunted,' she said. 'It feels as though some curse has been put on it. So many unpleasant things are happening.'

He remained silent for a while, then started, 'I'm sorry . . .'

'Not your fault.'

'About not telling you I mean, that Cathy was blind.'

'Yes,' she said, having forgotten it seemed, 'why didn't you tell me?'

He shrugged his shoulders. Suddenly he didn't want to discuss it.

'Because she gets all the sympathy?' Natalie suggested.

He nodded. She was so astute.

'I can understand that,' she said. 'But if you had told me, it would have explained a lot more about you than I figured. I misjudged you.'

'In what way?' He was surprised.

'I thought you were spoilt.'

'Well, I suppose I am.'

'Oh no. Her parents have been buying your services in order not to be responsible for her. You've been paying a very high price for your so-called freedom.'

She was right. He had wanted to love Cathy and make the marriage a success, but it had become impossible.

'Your parents-in-law, by the way, are with her in the manager's office, and I should be there too. I want to keep you out of all this as much as possible.' She fished something out of a drawer. 'Here's the key to my room. I want you to slip along there unnoticed and stay there until I join you, which may not be for another two or three hours. OK? There's some snacks in the fridge behind the door and plenty to drink.'

'What if they ask where I am?'

'I'll just say that you disappeared. You had absolutely nothing to do with the tragedy. The only people who need to see you are the police, for confirmation that you're Cathy's husband . . . but otherwise the more scarce you make yourself the better.'

He went along to her room, put on all the lights and sat down on the sofa.

He then got up and went to the fridge and helped himself to a glass of cold white wine.

The hotel haunted? She was mad. And Cathy was mad.

A phrase came into his head. Two saxophones and a violin holding a high note. Strange. Saxophones.

Playing modern music would either corrupt the purity of his composition, or enhance it!

Natalie watched Donald leave the office with her key. But for the grace of God he could now have been lying on the bed in Room 101 under a white sheet, like Charlie.

She downed a measure of brandy and corked the bottle hard. PRs did become alcoholics but she had never thought there was a chance in hell of that happening to her. Now she wasn't sure.

How? How to tell Martineau and Edgars that upstairs in Room 1510 Felix was lying dead?

She went along the corridor to the main office and walked in. Cathy was sitting in one of the armchairs, totally composed, a glass of iced water in her hand. Natalie didn't know whether she knew that Charlie had died, or indeed that she had murdered the wrong man, but certainly her face was as calm as a mask. The parents, on the other hand, were sitting on the edge of the sofa nervously changing expressions, not knowing at all what society expected of them in such a situation.

Edgars was standing in one corner. Martineau was behind his desk.

'We're waiting for the police,' Martineau said quietly.

'Would you like me to go down to reception and meet them?' she suggested.

'Hopefully they'll come in the back way. I did request that they should.'

'I'd best go down,'

The police were in fact discretion itself, so much so that when she got down to the staff entrance she nearly passed them, a Detective Inspector and a Detective Sergeant in unassuming plain clothes.

She took them up in the lift to the first floor, exchanged banalities about the newness of the hotel, did not talk of the event at all and led them to Martineau's office.

Before entering the Detective Inspector suggested that he would like to talk to the manager first to get a picture of what had happened. So instead she showed them into the Earl's Bar which was closed, and rang for Martineau after offering them both a drink.

The Detective Inspector was a cultured man in his early fifties who could well have been a guest. Scotland Yard did not just send anyone who was available but obviously chose the man most suitable, even his Detective Sergeant had a young executive air about him so that both blended in with the sophisticated surroundings.

Martineau came in looking unsettled, and when questioned repeated what he had been told had happened. The Inspector then asked Natalie for her version which was exactly the same and, satisfied that he had a rough enough idea of what he was dealing with, requested an office or room where he could interview the house detective, the head waiter, other staff, witnesses and then Cathy and her parents.

Natalie suggested her own office and as they made their way there, a young uniformed police officer, cap in hand, reported for duty.

'Did you come through main reception?'

'Yes, sir.'

'Were you not told to report round the back?'

'No, sir.'

The Detective Inspector sighed then told him to go and stand just inside Martineau's office and not let the young woman out of his sight.

Once the law had settled themselves down in the PR office, Martineau invited Natalie back to have a drink in the Earl's Bar where he sat very silent and deep in thought.

'This isn't going to do our image too much good,' he said drinking back his whisky.

'No,' she agreed.

She filled his glass up with another double, helped herself to her fifth glass of brandy, and took a deep breath.

'I've another shock for you.'

He looked at her, his eyes a little glazed, his expression definitely weary.

'There's another death, in Room 1510.'

'Who?'

'Felix Pearsall.'

'The journalist? Friend of yours?'

'Acquaintance, yes.'

'And he's dead? What did he die of?'

'Heart failure?'

'When?'

'Shortly after the disaster in the Panorama.'

'Doctor seen him?'

'Not yet.'

She told him everything as it had happened, her fears of Felix getting to his paper with the murder story, him telephoning, the falling forward onto the floor, dead.

themselves her blindness was due to disease. They were people who had nothing to fall back on at all but money, and that, sometimes, was not enough.

He had got what he wanted. Peace of mind for a while to compose. Then he had failed them. He had tried the impossible – to make them understand his music. Even if they had heard a composition of his on the radio with a full orchestra it would have meant absolutely nothing to them. All they knew of the classics was *The Mikado*, *Swan Lake* and the *Blue Danube*. They did not even own a record player.

His one night of glory at the Wigmore Hall, playing his own composition, had been disastrous. They had bought up the first row for themselves and friends and turned it into a social occasion. Over and above everyone he had heard his father-in-law talk and people had shushed, and he had seen Cathy shrink with embarrassment, her hearing being more acute than anyone else's.

He understood why she had wanted to kill him. She was the only one who understood his work. To hear him playing in the Panorama Room was tantamount to sacrilegious desecration. Her fury had been the fury of the purist whose purity had been violated.

'I've got hold of the best lawyer, of course, and I'm going round to see him at eleven,' father-in-law said. 'Now that you're here I think it might be useful if you came along.'

He knew what it meant. He would sit in the lawyer's office knowing how simply everything could be explained, but having to listen to everything being complicated out of all proportion because subtleties in an exchange of views were never grasped.

But he had to go.

They left after he had shaved and changed his clothes. Mother-in-law did not say another word to him, a brief look told him what she thought. It was his fault that her daughter was mad, as it was his fault that she had gone blind ten years before he knew her. They were people who were incapable of shouldering their own responsibilities.

The lawyer listened to Cathy's father's story with great

patience, and Donald listened too, not believing that anyone could lie to himself so convincingly. It was not Cathy who had wielded the knife, it was not Cathy who had crossed the dance floor to attack the pianist, it seemed he was going to convince himself that Cathy hadn't been there at all.

The lawyer glanced at him several times and then made it quite clear that there was little he could do until he had studied the police report and witnesses' statements.

'If I may call on your time in the next few days, Mr Southam, I'd be grateful.'

Though his daughter was in custody and his wife was alone at home worrying in her way about the consequences of the tragedy, he was able to suggest a lunch at his club.

Donald watched him eat heartily and drink heartily and he did not mention the matter once. The *Times*' leader about the Prime Minister's latest move regarding the economy, the fact that a certain horse had run well in some handicap, the mocking of a friend's stupidity at selling a house below its market value, all these were discussed and it was not until they were in the coffee room being served coffee and a brandy that the subject was finally broached. The future.

What did he, Donald, think would happen?

She would be let out on bail, under surveillance, possibly a nurse to look after her. She might be pronounced insane and sent to an asylum.

'Best thing for her,' the man commented, 'if she has gone mad. And what are you going to do now?' he asked before Donald could recover.

'Move out,' he replied.

He hadn't thought about it at all, it had not even occurred to him that the question would be asked so soon.

'Where to? You have no money to move out, to live elsewhere.'

'I'll manage, thank you.'

To which there was no reply.

He knew he had just lost a great deal, but Natalie's advice was ringing in his ears. 'It's got to the point where you've got to save yourself first or everyone else will sink with you.

Leave, get strong, then come back and help if you can.'

Back at the house, after a silent taxi ride, he packed the largest suitcase he could find with everything that fitted into it, not caring too much about personal belongings after cramming in most of his sheet music. Pyjamas, tooth brush and electric shaver he remembered, two suits and a dinner jacket and several shirts. He didn't take any of his records, none of his books, he just locked the case and left his and Cathy's apartment, left the house and walked all the way up the street to the hotel.

He went in through the staff entrance, past the security guard, who knew him. He went up in the lift to the first floor and let himself into Natalie's room.

He sat down exhausted, then, realizing just how tired he was, and decided to try and get some sleep. He lay down on her bed after drawing the curtains, but his mind started searching for anxieties. Natalie was a generous girl and he was taking advantage of her, which he didn't like, but then right now he had to. What he didn't have to do, however, was think about it, so he returned to the living room, opened the fridge and a cupboard, found a glass, poured himself a drink and added a number of ice cubes. A vodka and tonic. Alcohol would help him forget.

He went back to bed, stretched a hand out and turned on the radio. To his astonishment the station was broadcasting piano music, the very piece Charlie had been playing when Cathy had attacked him. It was being played more slowly, rather as he might play it, and behind the music he thought he could hear the sound of breathing. It was not very distinct, but it was there.

Could it be that someone was playing upstairs in the Panorama and it was being relayed through the audio system?

He had to go and see.

He took a lift to go up, but when the doors closed after he'd pressed the top button, the lift went down, one of the hazards of this great computerised world.

He waited patiently, watching the indicator lights flash on above the door.

He was taken down to the basement, right down to the lowest floor and the doors opened. Standing against a white tiled wall of the kitchen area was a strange looking old man he had never seen before. He was very pale, yellow skinned, bald, with deep set eyes. He was beckoning, suggesting, Donald supposed, that he should come out of the lift to let him in.

So he politely stepped out.

One strange thing he noticed about himself since coming to the hotel was how his manners had improved. Everything in such elegant surroundings was done with the minimum of noise and the maximum of politeness.

He smiled at the old man, more or less waved him into the lift, but the doors closed before the old man could move.

'I'll get it for you . . .' Donald said, pressing the button.

The man shook his head and beckoned him to follow.

Was something wrong? Did he need help?

The old man led the way down the white tiled passage to the kitchens proper, which were deserted except for a chef frying something over one of the cookers.

The man looked behind him occasionally to make sure Donald was still there, then stopped in front of the massive refrigerator doors. He held out his hand as much as to say 'Please open it for me.'

Donald pulled open the heavy door and the man stepped into the cold atmosphere, then through a second heavy door into an even colder room where sides of beef and pork were hanging in rows from steel rails, and tray upon tray of cooked meats were stacked on shelves.

The man lifted his eyebrows and smiled, then playfully darted behind one of the beef carcasses.

Donald was nonplussed, and quite suddenly aware of the extreme cold.

Then the lights went out.

He stayed quite still for a moment, listened for the man's movements and called out, 'Are you there? Are you all right?'

There was total silence. There was no sound, and it frightened him.

Fearing the old man might panic, or worse catch his death in the extreme cold, he tried to retrace his steps in the dark to the door but he bumped into the sides of meat, then heard them rattling along the rails as though they were being pushed.

'Is this a game?'

There was a muffled laugh, hardly audible, but it was there. He moved and again bumped into the sharp hard frozen bones of a carcass.

He didn't like it at all and the cold air burned down his throat.

As the sides were moved along the steel rails again he put out his hands to ward off anything that might hit him, then suddenly, quite suddenly, his hands were cut violently with something which swished through the dark.

He screamed.

He fell to the floor on his knees, the lights came on, and when he looked down he saw that two fingers of his left hand and three fingers of his right had been severed.

CHAPTER SIX

Natalie visited Donald in the hospital.

He was in a private room, sedated, pale but seemingly comfortable.

'I'm not going to stay here for ever, you know,' he said.

'Two days more, the doctors recommend, then you can move to my flat in Baron's Court. The person I had staying there is moving out. I don't want you back at the hotel.'

He held up his bandaged hands.

'It seems my new brilliant career as bar pianist has ended.'

'Your career is composing. This won't stop you, and they can do wonders with plastic surgery and mechanical devices.'

'The stubs hurt when I think of playing.'

'Then don't think of playing.'

She promised she would visit him again in the afternoon, then took a cab to the King's Road where, two years ago, as a giggle, she had gone to a palmist to have her future read. The palmist had predicted enormous wealth and success in a new direction which, though she had never admitted it to anyone, had encouraged her to apply for the Palace Plaza job which she otherwise would not have even considered. That was where palm reading and tarot cards could help, jarring the mind into thinking in new and unthought of directions.

She had liked the woman, had had confidence in her and knew that she wouldn't be laughed at, for she was beginning to have doubts about her own sanity. She was not certain enough that what was happening at the hotel could be a form of psychic manifestation. Though she had seen an apparition herself and there was certainly evidence that unaccountable occurrences were totting up, to believe that Robert Clariss,

Felix and Charlie had died as a result of a haunting was asking too much of anyone's credulity. As far as anyone else was concerned, Robert and Felix had died of heart failure, Charlie had been stabbed by a neurotic blind woman and Donald, suffering some sort of mental breakdown as a result of his wife's lunatic behaviour, had accidentally locked himself up in the cold room and hurt himself badly on something sharp when trying to get out.

The old man in the Panorama Bar could be imagination, though he had apparently been seen by others. The one really inexplicable incident was the behaviour of those knives during the children's party which everyone had preferred to forget.

So she'd decided that before doing anything more positive about it all, she would wait for further developments, if there were going to be any, in fact begging the ghost to prove it existed in a more concrete form. What she had chosen to ignore, of course, was Donald's version of what had happened to him, and the coincidence of the radio music.

The evening Donald lost his fingers she had been in the Suzerain Suite seeing to the setting up of a Cable Television conference when Tania had asked to speak to her for a moment.

'Something strange is happening to the audio system in all suites and rooms.'

'How do you mean?'

'Come and listen.'

They had gone to an empty third floor room and switched on the radio. On all channels there had been piano music, 'Mood Indigo', the very tune that had been played when Charlie was attacked.

'The electricians have been working on it for an hour, they've checked everything, but can't make it out. They've even switched off the system altogether and pulled out the fuses, but it still gets piped through.'

It was three in the afternoon. She'd gone up alone to the Panorama Restaurant and as she'd entered through the glass swing doors she'd heard the piano being played and in a way had been relieved thinking that Donald was perhaps practising and by some fault somewhere it had been relayed.

She'd stood just inside the door behind a mirrored column so that she could not be seen, had closed the doors quietly, leaned against them and listened to the playing till it had stopped.

She'd moved a little forward and to one side to see if it was him, but there had been no one there.

No one was sitting at the piano, there was no one standing by it, no one anywhere near it, and the only way out of the room unobserved would have been through the plate glass windows.

She'd felt very cold indeed, turned, and had run down the corridor to the stairs.

The fear of ghosts had got to her.

Shortly after, in her office, Sister had rung through on the house phone to tell her that Donald had been found unconscious in one of the kitchen freezers, his hands mutilated, and that she was having him sent to hospital.

Madame Raymonda, clairvoyant, was alone in her tiny booth in the basement of the Chelsea Bargains Market between an Indian sari stall and a leather jacket concession.

She was behind black nylon curtains knitting a small blue cardigan for a child. Natalie sat down on a small stool in front of her and waited.

'You don't mind if I finish this row dear, do you? It's for my little granddaughter, a Virgo she is, ever so sweet, my son's little girl. He married a Spanish lady you know, and they go down there, to Spain, so I don't see them too often.'

Natalie watched the needles tick away and the row come to an end.

'I suppose I should be doing it in pink, but she's got ever such clear blue eyes I thought I'd make it match. What would you like then, the crystal? The cards or the palm? I do all three . . . but then you've been here before haven't you?'

'Yes.'

'I remember you. You're an Aquarian and do Public Relations work, you've changed jobs though haven't you, you're working with a lot of people now, I can see that, and you're concerned about something quite serious.'

The woman took her palm and looked at it, then looked up at her.

'You had two options when I last saw you . . . way back. You still have two options, only they've changed.'

'What are they?'

'They're very strange lines, dearie. Would you like to tell me what you've really come about?'

'I don't want to sound silly, but I think the place I work in is haunted, and I'd like someone to confirm this.'

'Where is it that you work?'

'May I tell you that later? I would like to know whether you can recommend anyone who is psychic enough to tell me whether I'm right.'

'Would you like me to come?'

'Of course.'

'Is it far?'

'It's the new London Palace Plaza Hotel.'

The woman didn't seem surprised. She checked her watch.

'It's time I closed anyway. Business is very bad these days. What tube station is near, dear? I have to get back to Victoria. I live in Worthing you see, only come up three days a week.'

As Natalie followed her up the stairs and walked out into the King's Road to hail a taxi, she assured Madame Raymonda that a hotel car would take her to whatever station she wanted to go.

The palmist talked non-stop all the way to the hotel, chatting about the price she'd had to pay that morning for her cat food, about a leak in the roof of the bungalow left her by her husband, about her son and his Spanish wife. It was reassuring in a way, not once did she ask any personal questions but took her clairvoyance as part of everyday life.

When she stepped out of the taxi and looked up at the tall magnificence of the Palace Plaza however, she smiled knowingly at Natalie.

'Oh I can feel the vibrations from here my dear. I don't even have to go in. You're absolutely right. There's something very strong manifesting itself in there.'

Natalie, who had intended telling her everything that had happened, now decided not to say anything at all. She just led the way up the marble steps and in through the revolving doors.

Madame Raymonda stopped in the middle of the main foyer and closed her eyes. She stood quite still for a few seconds, then moved on, up the wide stairs and down the corridor to the main PR office where she again stopped.

'Do you know anything about the site on which this hotel was built?' she asked.

'No.'

'It would be interesting to find out what was here before. A number of people have passed over to the other side from here recently, haven't they?'

'Yes,' Natalie opened her office door. 'Please come in. Would you like some tea, buttered toast, cakes? We have everything.'

'Scones with Devonshire cream and blackcurrant jam would be very welcome.'

'Please make yourself comfortable.'

She left Madame Raymonda to go and organize tea. When she returned the clairvoyant was sitting well back in the arm chair, her finger tips together, her eyes down in contemplation, a frown creasing her forehead.

'I'm not welcome here,' she said, looking up. 'I'm getting that very clearly. There are perturbed spirits about, quite a few, who do not want me around. They are telling me to go.' She stood up suddenly.

'But you can't go!'

'Oh my dear I know when I'm not wanted, and I never stay unless I am.'

'But your tea . . .'

'I doubt whether I'd be allowed to drink it. I really should leave very quickly.'

'At least allow me to buy you a tea somewhere else?' Natalie suggested.

'Oh yes, by all means, but not here. Not here.'

So saying she picked up her bag and left the room very hurriedly, Natalie following.

They went down the road to a little cafe where scones and Devonshire cream would not be available but where Madame

Raymonda settled down more happily.

'My dear, that was quite an experience! The last time I felt such vibrations was when my husband died. It was the beginning of my career as an occultist as a matter of fact. I knew he was going to die you see, long before he actually did. Well, some weeks before, and I knew how.'

She paused, as though expecting her to ask how he had died, but Natalie wasn't sure she should, so looked even more interested, leaning forward in her seat across the small table.

'It was nothing very dramatic. He had a heart attack and died in his sleep, but for several days running previous to that not only did the three clocks in the house all stop at exactly the same hour, seventeen minutes past eleven, but I saw him lying there on the bed, laid out, when he was actually out at work. After he died, of course, I saw him sitting in his favourite chair waving at me, like I saw the two old men and the old woman at your hotel.'

'What two old men and old woman?'

'I don't know who they are my dear, but they are the people haunting the place. Of course in such an establishment there might be so many more.'

'Are they . . . evil?' Natalie asked.

'Probably.'

'What should I do?'

'To exorcise them you mean?'

'Yes . . .'

'Well, don't bring in a priest or a so-called exorcist, that's all a lot of mumbo jumbo. What you have to do is some research to find out how they came to be there and why they're staying.'

'But where do I start? Do they want something, do you think?'

'In my experience, and in this area I don't have too much, there are three types of hauntings. Revenants who were unhappy in a place and return to purge it. Revenants who were happy in a place and return because they like the surroundings, and revenants who need something from that particular place. These are the most complex, for one can never guess what they are seeking. They are also the greatest nuisance for they tend to be restless and sometimes even mischievous.'

'Three people have died of unnatural causes. Would you call that mischievous?'

'Oh, death is nothing terrible to them, you see. It's rather like tripping someone over to see them fall into a puddle, I suppose. They know it's not the end. It's only us mortals who are afraid of dying as we fear everything unknown.'

'How can I communicate with them?'

'Best not to try, my dear, though they'll communicate with you if they so wish. But you must do two things. First find out the history of the site on which the hotel was built, then you should check through the list of the people who are living in the hotel at present, for one of them may hold the key to the problem. Do you have any religious people staying there, for instance?'

'Not now. Carmel Dreihardt was with us a few days.'

'See if there's any connection dear, between the date of his stay and any of the passing overs, or manifestations I expect you've had.'

'We have had some manifestations,' Natalie confirmed.

But Madame Raymonda was not interested. That was something she had taken for granted.

Natalie watched her eat through two buttered crumpets and two cup cakes, and drink down three cups of tea, during all of which she had talked non-stop about her life in Worthing, her favourite television programmes, her dog and her cats. It was hard to believe that this woman had psychic knowledge and lived such a humdrum life, though once, during her monologue, Natalie had to stop her to check what she was talking about.

'I was chatting to Elma, only the other day,' she was saying, 'and she was telling me about the animals on the other side.'

Natalie was not sure whether the other side was a garden fence or death.

'The other side of life, my dear. Elma died twelve years ago but I'm in constant contact with her. She's very happy.'

'How do you speak to her?'

'On the telephone, my dear. It's by far the clearest way.'

'You dial a number?' she ventured. She nearly wanted to laugh.

'Oh no. You just lift the receiver and she comes through. She knows when I want to have a natter. Anyway, Elma was saying that she had seen MacFido, he was my husband's little Scotch terrier when I first met him. Now I wanted Humphrey to know that MacFido was with him, but of course I've never been able to contact Humphrey.'

'Why not?'

'If only I knew! You have to accept certain things about the other side, the main one being that there are no rules. Or if there are they are never communicated to us on this plane.'

She looked at her watch and became worried about catching her train.

'How much do I owe you?' Natalie asked.

'Oh . . . five pounds my dear, it's what I would have charged you for a palm reading.'

'Are you sure that's enough? I've taken up a lot of your time and it will go down on expenses. Let's say ten.'

'Just as you wish,' Madame Raymonda said, taking the ten pound note and thrusting it in her bag.

Natalie paid the bill at the till and followed her into the street and hailed a taxi.

'Here's another three pounds for the taxi fare.'

As she got into the cab Madame Raymonda took Natalie's hand and squeezed it gently. 'There is just one thing I'd like to know. Is there someone in your life at the moment connected with music?'

'Yes . . . there is.'

'Well my dear, while talking to you I've had these very strong vibrations connected with that person. They're all around you, especially when we were in the hotel. They're not good. So be careful.'

'What do you mean, they're not good?'

Madame Raymonda was in the taxi, she closed the door and lowered the window as the cab was about to move off.

'They're not good within the hotel. You must perhaps not see that person there, the two do not go together. He is going to suffer and you must help him. You must help him for your own sake.' The taxi drew away.

Donald stood outside the Earls Court Road police station and paused before going in.

Pending a directive from the Home Office, Cathy was being held. She was a special case, blind, needing assistance in certain things so could not be treated like other prisoners awaiting trial.

He had come from Natalie's flat where she had insisted he should stay after coming out of hospital. She had been so emphatic about this that she had asked her tenant to leave in a hurry, had come to collect him at the hospital and settled him in, not accepting any words of protest. She had her reasons, she'd told him, why he shouldn't come to visit her at the hotel.

'The management?' he'd queried.

'No . . .' she'd answered with hesitation, then had asked him whether he believed in ghosts.

'Why?'

She told him that she thought the hotel might be haunted and had recounted what she had experienced.

'I think it all makes quite a lot of sense. I am slightly psychic myself,' he'd admitted.

She'd looked at him astonished. 'Why didn't you say so before?'

'For the same reason that you've never mentioned the haunting idea before. These are things that the majority of people laugh at and I don't like being laughed at.'

'What makes you think you are psychic?'

'An experience.'

'Oh come on, Donald, tell me. I need to understand. Something strange is happening in the hotel and I must conquer it.'

And he'd told her, about the time when he was in a rehearsal at the London College of Music and Drama, in one of the tiny rooms at the top of the building which had just enough room for an upright piano and a chair. He had been practising scales and a piece by Schumann prior to going down to have his lesson with Mr Tibbings, when the professor himself had come into the room and stood over him, watching him play, and then told him that he would have to cancel the lesson today due to unforeseen circumstances. There had been absolutely nothing unusual about his coming in like that, he had been wearing the same old tweed suit he always wore, with the same old check shirt and woollen tie, but as he had closed the door Donald had noticed that two fingers of his left hand and three of his right were missing, which was impossible as Tibbings played the piano beautifully. A trick of light, a temporary mental aberration on his part. He hadn't thought much of it till that afternoon when he had been stopped by a fellow student in the canteen. Had he heard about Tibbings? The old man had died that morning at about the time he had been visited by him in the rehearsal room.

'And the missing fingers?' Natalie had asked, 'A premonition, do you think?'

'Seems like it,' he'd said.

He walked into the police station and at the desk asked to see Cathy, explaining who he was. It took time for him to be cleared, telephone calls to superiors were made, confirmed by others till he was eventually shown up to a small room on the second floor which he presumed was a cell.

She was sitting, as was her manner, on the edge of the narrow bed, feet and knees together, hands clasped in her lap. She looked no different except that she did not wear her dark glasses and her small staring eyes made her blindness obvious immediately.

He sat down next to her and put his hand on hers.

'I didn't want to harm you,' she said.

'I know.'

'It wasn't me that did it. Can you understand that?'

'I can believe it, but it would be better if you tried to explain what happened?'

'I saw, Donald, I saw! There were three of them in the middle of the dance floor. The parquet flooring was of white satin wood, the curtains pink, panorama windows all around overlooking London. It was quite beautiful. I saw the five-piece band, I saw all the guests, not dressed in dinner jackets as I had imagined, but dressed anyhow, some men even without ties . . . that was one surprise. The three people in the middle of the floor were correctly dressed, the two men in dinner jackets, the old woman in an evening gown, grey and white. It was she who beckoned to me, came right up to me and held out her hands and I got up and took them. They were strange hands to feel, as though they weren't there at all, as though I was just holding out my hands in the air.'

'Weren't you surprised that you could see, so suddenly?'

'No . . . I thought it quite natural,' Cathy said, then after a reflective pause: 'One of the old men then picked up a carving knife from the meat trolley which was close by, took a napkin from a waiter as well I remember, and he placed the knife on the napkin and held it out to me, presenting it to me like a sword of honour on a Royal hassock.'

Her brow puckered a little as she remembered what followed.

'I knew what to do, instinctively. The woman stepped backwards in a half curtsy, indicating the pianist. I crossed the room, the three of them close behind. I held the knife at hip level, not like a dagger but as though . . . as though I were holding a torch. I knew I had to aim at an area under the heart, knew that that is what I should do . . . but at the moment of striking . . . I went blind again and I had no idea what I was doing. I just felt the knife go in, and heard the screams. After that . . . confusion . . . I felt something wet on my hands, I heard father shouting at me, mother scolding me . . . "What do you think you're doing?" It was what she said at the time of the accident. That was all she ever said wasn't it. "What do you think you're doing?" '

He tightened his grip on her hands, not wanting her to live through that event again. She had suffered it enough times, had woken him up in the middle of the night reliving the accident. It sounded so stupid and yet so simple. It was a hot summer when she was seven, at the country house with the new swimming pool, during a house party with fashionable friends. Nanny was away, which had irritated her mother because she couldn't be bothered with the child. There had been a lot of organization going on in the morning and father had discovered the pool was not very clean, the water not as clear as it should be, with little insects swimming about round the edge. Furious, he had gone to the garden shed and found some chemical which he'd thought was for the pool and had poured it in to kill the animals. She had been in her swim suit, had just learned to dive and was looking forward to the party to show people how well she could swim under water.

'Can I go in now Daddy?'

She had dived in, eyes wide open, through a cloud of the chemical, and it had burned.

She had come out, screaming, but some important guest had arrived at precisely the same moment and neither mother nor father could cope, so they had taken her upstairs quickly, bathed her eyes with water and told her to go and lie down in her room in the dark till the pain had gone. She hadn't been able to see and the pain was fearful and she had made her way to the top of the stairs, no longer screaming, but crying, and she had called out and her mother hadn't come. She had gone down the stairs, through the drawing room and into the garden, bumping several times against the furniture till eventually someone who knew her had taken her by the hand.

'What are you doing, Catherine?' her mother's severe voice had asked in her darkness. 'Go and play!'

'I can't see, mother.'

'Of course you can see. Children always find ways of getting attention the moment Nanny's away. It really is most inconvenient of her . . .' And she had been led back up to the nursery and told to be a good girl and stop play-acting. And she had stayed there for an hour or so, in great pain, till a kind woman with a kind voice had come in and asked, 'Don't you like parties either?' and she had said, 'I can't see,' and the woman had been very sympathetic and heard the story out after which she had left her for a moment then everyone had come rushing in and father had picked her up and put her in the car and driven her to the doctor who had declared that it was probably too late . . .

'Why did you come to the hotel?' Donald asked.

'Mother and father wanted me to hear you play for myself. They heard you were there from friends who go there often. They don't want to support you anymore, you see. They wanted to prove to me that you weren't worthy of all the attention they have given you and all the money they've spent on you.'

She paused and squeezed his hand. 'What do you think will happen to me now, Donald?'

'I don't think much. You'll be all right. It'll be unpleasant for a while, but they'll let you off, maybe a year or so on probation.'

'You'll leave me, won't you? You'll go with that other woman?'

'What other woman?' he protested.

'I don't know her name, I know nothing about her, but there is another woman of whom you're very fond. I can tell Donald, you know I can tell.'

It was impossible.

He tightened his grip on her hands without meaning to, then disengaged himself, realizing it was the wrong thing to do.

God . . . he was trapped. He disliked her parents for their insensitivity but had to admit that sometimes he understood their plight. With the blind depending on you, you were caught for ever, you were tied.

'I won't mind if they put me away. It'll make very little difference. I would like a musical instrument to play though, the oboe perhaps. I could learn to play the oboe to perfection.'

'I don't think they'll put you away, Cathy. You can hardly be considered a danger.'

He was told he had to leave by a policewoman. He looked back at Cathy, sitting there as he had found her. She could sit like that for hours.

'What happened to your hands Donald?' she asked, without turning her face.

'I had an accident.'

'The three old people?' she asked.'

'What three old people?'

But before she could answer the police woman asked him to leave again.

'I'll tell you when we next meet.'

He walked up Earls Court Road to Kensington High Street

and along past all the shops. It was good to be among human beings again.

He paused outside a record shop and looked at the display of classical records. There was the LP of Bortkievich's Piano Concerto in B-Flat Major, Opus Sixteen which he had left at the house along with all his collection. Natalie had a good hi-fi system in her flat; it would calm him down enormously to have his records with him, so he decided to go and get them.

He walked all the way, turned down Palace Gate Terrace looking up at the Palace Plaza which dwarfed all the other surrounding buildings. It was a beautiful piece of architecture, one of the few modern constructions he enjoyed looking at. He walked on down to the house and let himself in.

As soon as he closed the front door his father-in-law came out of the drawing room. He could never get to the stairs without being summoned to pay allegiance.

The man looked sombre and pale. 'Can you come in a moment?'

He went in, and stood just inside the door.

'Sit down Donald.'

The use of his Christian name augured badly. Had a major decision affecting him been taken? But Cathy's mother was sitting in an unusual corner crying, a handkerchief to her nose.

'We've just heard from the police station . . . Cathy has died.'

'But I just left her!'

'Oh, we know that!' Came a biting accusation from the mother. 'We know that! What we don't know is what you said to her.'

'What happened?' he asked, though he didn't have to. He could guess. She had killed herself. Somehow she had managed to kill herself.

'The moment you left . . . she escaped from her cell and ran out into the street.'

'How could she?'

'We don't know. She asked to be taken to the bathroom, and escaped the warder, who quite clearly wasn't looking after her properly. Somehow she made her way to the street and threw herself in front of a bus.'

He could imagine the scene. She would have known by the sounds, would have chosen a heavy vehicle.

The accusing litany went on, but he didn't listen. This is what they had been waiting for, for twenty years, the tragedy that would put an end to their guilt. They had got rid of their daughter and it was not their fault. Either the police were guilty or he was guilty, but not them.

He stood up and walked out of the room. At the door he paused. 'I'm going to take all my belongings now and leave altogether.'

As he started up the stairs he heard Cathy's mother declare, 'I told you he always wanted her dead.'

For one whole week nothing happened.

After arranging Charlie's cremation Natalie negotiated on behalf of his widow for compensation and a pension. It was hard work, convincing the widow that despite her admirable principals of not wanting to make money out of her husband's death it was her due and the company should pay up. It was just as hard convincing Martineau that though Charlie had not been a regular employee his widow should receive something, but she won the day by simply turning the whole affair into another good image-making occasion for the hotel. The company publicly gave the woman a generous cheque and a picture of her receiving it was in all the trade magazines which pleased the board no end.

Donald meanwhile stayed in her flat, emerging once for Cathy's funeral, a bizarre affair in a country churchyard. Her parents had apparently donated a quite large sum of money towards the repairs of the ecclesiastic roof so that their daughter would be buried in consecrated ground without it being made known that she was a murderess and a suicide. It mattered to the vicar, apparently, who had archaic powers to refuse.

She sat with Donald in a back pew and afterwards helped him escape the Press who were anxious to get a picture of the husband the deceased had failed to kill.

He was pleased to see her, grateful for the loan of her flat but obviously quite anxious and, understandably, unsettled.

'My sister has invited me to stay in Wales for a week or two. The rest away from it all would do me good, but would you mind?'

She assured him that because she had lent him her flat it did not mean that he owed her explanations about his life, and the following day she saw him off on the train at Paddington station, relieved that he was going far away and giving her time to sort out her feelings about him.

It was by chance that she then got him some work.

A film unit had booked the Panorama Restaurant for an early morning shoot of the London rooftops at dawn and she was up there drinking coffee with the director when the producer called in. He was an American of consequence, young and frightening in his aggressiveness. The film was to be based on the life of a virtuoso violinist and she casually asked him who was arranging the music, and he said that he had not yet chosen anyone. He was a music buff himself, a composer of sorts, failed, and he needed someone who understood the modern classics with whom he could have a complete rapport. She mentioned Donald Southam as a possibility, adding that he was in the country right now working on a composition, but the producer took his address and phone number and said he would contact him.

A week later, to her surprise, she got a call from an excited Donald saying that the producer had visited him and that after showing him some of his scores the man had asked him to submit a theme for the film for which he would be paid an incredible sum of money.

Two weeks after that she got another excited call from him explaining that he was being flown to New York to work with sound film technicians on the film score, and then she received a letter from Hollywood, no less, a big thank you, promising that he would come and stay at the hotel as soon as he returned, begging her to understand that while the going was good he had to abandon her. What had interested the producer, apparently, was the fact that he had been through such a terrible experience which made itself felt in his music, what was more, the violinist in the film lost the use of his hands towards the end. The letter went on, 'Before leaving I read the biographies of Scott Fitzgerald and Eleanor Parker and thought it would be impossible for me, but I do not seem to be touched by the things that matter to other people. I am not after a fortune, simply a way to forget the recent past, except you. I have sat through countless old movies to listen to the scores and now know what it is all about. What it is about is really confidence, then it is easy. I will be coming back to London to work with the orchestra and trust that I will see you . . . often.'

Meanwhile, awaiting his return, awaiting his success, aware that she felt she owned part of him, or wanting to, regretting that their brief relationship had not developed more, she busied herself clearing the name of the hotel and trying hard to get news stories that were happy and youthful.

A few film stars came to stay, she organized an exhibition of photographic nudes which caused some interest and the board did not expect much more from her.

There were no sinister events or manifestations for six weeks and she allowed the file on the hotel's history to slowly slip down in the in-tray.

At first she had thought she was onto something truly unpleasant when she had started looking into the history of the site. She had discovered that the accident rate among the building workers during the laying of the foundations had been high: five dead, nine badly injured and all on different occasions. The site, she learned, had been a National car park for three years before Euro-International had purchased it, and before that it had been a bomb site; the private residence dating back to George III which had once stood there had been damaged during the blitz. The walls which had withstood the bombs had collapsed one day onto three cars trapping the occupant of one and killing another. The debris had been cleared, the ruins pulled down and the area closed. She had found out very little to date about the house itself, Number 12 Palace Terrace, but she had had too little time to complete the research, having perhaps gone into the deaths of the workmen too thoroughly.

As the long period of peace extended itself she had filed her notes away, hoping that she would never have to refer to them again. Then Donald turned up, unexpectedly as always, a telephone message from reception informing her that he had booked into Suite 809 and requested her company if she was free.

She rang him immediately explaining that she was tied up with an optical instrument manufacturer's convention, but that she would join him as soon as possible, suggesting the Earl's Bar.

She went down and met him there and was pleasantly surprised, by the cut of his lightweight suit for a start, by his shoes, his casual air. His tan and the leather gloves hiding his mutilated hands were an incredible improvement in his appearance.

He was full of stories, he was alive, his blue eyes danced, confidence pulsating out of him. He preferred her with longer hair, he said, he liked the way she had had it curled. His 'little blonde' he called her, and he talked of all the people he had met, big names which hadn't meant a thing to him before, and he was astonished himself at how he had been able to forget Cathy. He even admitted that he had gone to stand outside the old house, which was up for sale, and had felt nothing at all, not a pang of regret. He had her to thank for that, for everything, for encouraging him before the fearful events and for looking after him and guiding him when it was over, not to mention her introduction of the producer.

He wanted to take her out to dinner, but she said she couldn't leave the hotel as it was Tania's night off, so he suggested a *tête-à-tête* dinner in the Panorama, which she was doubtful about as he hadn't been there since the night of Charlie's murder.

'To kill a ghost,' he said, full of confidence. So she went to change, putting on a new tan dress.

'It strikes me,' she said, as they were seated, looking out over London, 'that there's been a woman or two in your life recently.'

'One or two,' he admitted, smiling.

'It's done you good.'

'It taught me a thing or two.'

She raised her eyebrows.

Perhaps he had never slept with anyone but Cathy before, a virgin bridegroom married to his piano.

She glanced at her watch, excused herself and went down to the Monarch Suite to make sure that all was going well.

Back upstairs they had more champagne, brandy, and Donald asked her to dance. Donald Southam dancing disco! It was unbelievable, and funny. He had a quaint little movement with his feet, and he used his hands well, not shy of exposing the leather gloves, which brought attention. Then there was a slow, dreary number and he put his arms around her and hugged her. She felt pleasantly small in his arms, not vulnerable, but feminine, and he hugged her seductively, even lustily.

'I want you,' he whispered in one of her ears.

She said nothing. Did she want that now? Would it spoil the relationship, or was it inevitable?

Such a silly reaction. Of course she wanted to, she wanted to be with this man and to be loved by him.

'It'll cost you,' she whispered back.

'How much?'

'The price of another hotel room. I make it a rule never to sleep with anyone on my own doorstep.'

He pushed her away, pretending to look shocked.

'You do such things so often?'

She didn't like the rebuke from him, funnily, it made her feel cheap and she really regretted the remark.

'Very infrequently,' she said, 'but I am not celibate.'

'What hotel would you like?'

'At this time of night it might prove difficult.'

'You're putting up barriers.'

'No I'm not . . . but it is late.'

'And I want you, now!'

'I'll come to you then, but I'll have to leave before room service comes on duty.'

She deliberately ignored the sense of oppression she felt when she left her own suite, having gone there to change and put on suitable clothes for the morning in case she overslept, and when the lift took longer than usual to come up, she started to get worried. When the doors opened she saw the old man standing there inside it, smiling at her too benignly and she turned on her heels and ran up the stairs.

All the way up, a long way up, she felt frightened. She was not sure whether one of the others might not appear on the next landing, waiting there for her to remind her of all the distress she thought she had repulsed.

At the fifth landing she couldn't go on without a rest and decided to try the lift again. She would call the ghost's bluff, or face it.

She pressed the call button and it came down immediately. The lift doors opened, she steeled herself. It was empty.

Bravely, foolishly perhaps, she got in, pressed for the eighth floor and waited for disaster. The cables could be severed and she would be dropped to her death. The lift moved upwards, smoothly, the tiny bell rang and the doors opened.

Apprehensive, she waited before stepping out.

No one. Nothing. Not even the feeling of oppression.

Was it her imagination then, coupled with having drunk too much? Was it an association of ideas, a fear in her sub-conscious that Donald's presence in the hotel would bring the ghosts back?

She tapped gently on the door of 809 and it opened. She went in and Donald frightened her by grabbing hold of her from behind and kissing her passionately on the neck.

To her astonishment she realized he was completely nude except for his leather gloves, and dripping wet.

She turned and stepped back and looked at him in great surprise.

'Do you always receive your lady friends like this?'

'Always. It saves a great deal of embarrassment later.'

He had a nice looking body, tanned, and she tried not to look at his maleness too obviously but couldn't help it because he was excited already.

'You don't work up to things then?' she asked.

He was drying himself with a towel now.

'I was having a bath. Why don't you get back in with me?'

'We haven't even kissed!'

'Yes we have. Twice.'

'Twice is not enough.'

He grabbed hold of her again and this time kissed her on the mouth. It was very strange feeling, herself dressed against his naked male body and instinctively she reached down and found him and held him.

Without separating his mouth from hers he started to undress her, fumbling with the blouse buttons at the back, only one of which she had done up, purposefully. It was off, she was wearing no bra, and he cupped his hands over her breasts. It felt delightful, especially with his gloves.

When she was quite nude he picked her up bodily and took her to the bathroom where he immersed her slowly into the water, then got in behind her. He turned her round so that they faced each other then he suddenly took a deep breath and dived his head under the water to nestle it between her legs where he blew bubbles which tickled. He then came up just as suddenly staring at her with bright smiling eyes.

'You're mad!' she said, 'and obviously a repressed sex maniac.' Noticing his gloves she asked, 'Don't they get wet?'

'Yes. But I can't bear the sight of my fingers. Come on, I can't wait!'

She looked and it was clear that he couldn't, so she got out of the water and without bothering to dry herself led him to the bed and hurled herself onto it pulling him on top of her.

'If the hotel management knew how ill-treated their bed-clothes were they'd have a fit!' she said.

'Never mind how I treat the bedclothes, it's how I treat you that's going to upset them.'

And he was on her like a fiend, licking her ears, biting her lips, kissing her neck, her breasts, the line down her stomach to her navel and further, taking her hair between his teeth and tugging, hurting, caressing, mauling, adoring, till he slid himself up over her, into her and suffocated her with such a rhythmic passion that she smiled in the semi-darkness at the silly thought that this was always the way with musicians.

When it was all over and she was nestling under his arm he said in the night, in the safe darkness, 'Aren't you tired of living here in this artificial environment?'

'Yes . . .'

'Wouldn't you like to have a house in the country with trees and fields and walks to go on with the sun and the wind and the rain . . .'

'Yes.'

'I know of just such a place in the Welsh hills. It's beautiful and we could live there together and we could get married. Would you marry me?'

'Yes,' she said, wondering if she meant it, quite surprised but realizing that she would be happy to be with him.

'When can you leave here then?'

'Probably in a month,' she said slowly, 'but it would be fairer to say two.'

'That takes us up to August when the film will be finished. Marry me in August,' he said.

'OK.'

And as her mind clicked into a new gear, into a new future which she had never previously considered, she imagined herself flying with him to California, being able to help him in his career as she had already helped him, imagining a country house, herself looking after it, domesticity as it could be enjoyed, with him in his own studio room composing. As all these things went through her mind, she felt the temperature drop so much that she pulled the sheet over herself as he struggled to sit up and switch on the light.

'What's the matter?' she asked.

'I just felt terribly cold,' he explained.

Then he looked at her, stared at her curiously. 'You've gone quite pale.'

'Have I?' she whispered.

'You're afraid, aren't you?'

'A little bit.'

'First thing tomorrow I'm going to get you out of here. You can go on working if you want but I don't want you to sleep here. As from tomorrow we go to the flat to live together.'

Then the lights went out.

Through the window an eerie phosphorescence glowed.

They both got up, pulled back the curtains and found themselves staring at wisps of ectoplasm which were floating, dancing, in mid air, a few feet from the windows, as though beckoning them out.

CHAPTER SEVEN

Nightmares eventually come to an end, Natalie thought. They come to an end when you wake up.

But she was already wide awake, and so was Donald, and dawn was breaking.

She crossed the room to open the door. A bluish ecto-plasmic irridescence illuminated the corridor. She stepped back as it flickered, then went out.

Seconds later, in the semi-darkness, she felt something brush past her. She sensed a presence in front of her and behind her, neither more than three feet away, but invisible, and she slammed the door shut.

One of them, she felt, was in the room, but she turned and made straight for the telephone to call security.

The phone was dead.

Then, as soon as she replaced the receiver, the instrument rang.

'Thank God! Hallo?'

Not too long ago some pervert had rung her and breathed down the line. The first impression of the sound she now heard reminded her of this, but it was less human, it was a whine with endless echoes coming, it seemed, from a very great distance.

She put the receiver down and picked it up again,

It was still dead.

Then all the lights went on.

She looked at Donald, and there was an immediate understanding of what they should do. Wasting no time they both got dressed quickly, left the room and walked fast down the corridor, but as they did so every door of every room opened and out of each one stepped a grin.

She could not describe them any other way.

They were not people, nor forms, nor shapes. They were certainly not human. They were whitish with a face, eyes, long hair and dominated by a grinning mouth, an expression of mischievous evil.

The terrifying grins moved swiftly from one door to another, criss-crossing each other in a mad whirling pattern, and all the doors then slammed shut so loudly that seconds later some opened again and guests in pyjamas, nightshirts, in briefs and dressing gowns popped their heads out to enquire what the hell was going on.

There wasn't time to talk, to excuse, to explain, because the lights went out again. But not before Natalie realised that this was a show of supernatural force designed only for them. To the sleep-tousled guests the grins were invisible.

Natalie clasped Donald's hand tightly and more whooshed past her in the dark, a stream of them, the grins, touching her, freezing her arms, her legs, and they howled like banshees.

The lights went on again and the guests stood there in the corridor complaining, asking, demanding explanations.

Ignoring them Natalie started down the stairs.

'I don't want to risk the lifts,' she said.

'Eight floors!' Donald protested.

'Don't count. Let's just get out of here!'

She slid her hands down the bannister rail, jumping down two, three steps at a time, Donald close behind her.

They made it to the basement, rushed down the tiled passages, past the boiler house, Grant's office, towards the underground car park.

As they pushed open the last of the exit doors the ectoplasmic phosphorescence glowed threateningly around them again then faded as they went through and out, and ran up the steep slope towards the open air into the street.

Morning was breaking, all was incredibly fresh, incredibly peaceful.

They crossed the road, not talking, not wanting to discuss, not wanting to even look at the building they had just escaped from. Then Donald saw a taxi in the distance and ran towards it.

Natalie stood on the pavement alone for a while, daring to stare up at the towering magnificence of the new hotel, shining in all its glass and copper glory against the pale dawn sky. Then she gasped in horror as first one window panel shattered, then another, then another and misshapen human figures, like twisted rag dolls, were hurled out in the air to plummet helplessly down to the road below.

Eight victims in the space of a few seconds, impelled from different storeys by an unexplainable force to fearful death.

Donald gripped Natalie's hand as they stared in disbelief at the hideous sight of the strewn bodies in the street.

The most fearful aspect of it was that they lay on the road in a perfect semi-circle, as though they had been plucked at the moment of their fall and guided to a designated position.

'What is it?' Natalie whispered, 'what on earth can have so much power?'

The police arrived out of nowhere. The air was suddenly filled with sirens and bells. Five, seven, ten appliances arrived, police cars, police vans. A block was put up across the road.

'Move back please,' a policeman said.

Two of them were already closing off a large area with the familiar white emergency tape.

Some of the police, trying to get into the hotel through the main doors found them locked. Natalie could see the doorman inside battling with the mechanism and the locks.

She broke through the cordon.

'Miss! Miss!'

She was stopped, physically, an officer grabbing her by the arm.

'I'm staff,' she protested, 'try the back entrance, we got out that way.'

The policeman accompanied them both round the back and down into the garage to the metal swing doors leading into the basement corridors.

There was no more phosphorescence, no eeriness, a

strange peace in fact in the total silence.

They got ino the lift and when the doors opened at the first floor Martineau was standing there in the corridor with Derek Edgars.

'Thank God you're here,' he said, 'come on, I need you like I've never needed anyone before. It'll be a test of diplomacy and inventiveness to explain this one!'

She turned to Donald.

'I have to help out. I really do. Go to the flat and wait for me there. I'll ring you as soon as I possibly can.' And she followed Martineau into the main office.

Before the senior police investigators arrived to ask questions, she, Martineau and Edgars knew they had to come up with some sort of explanation for the incredible tragedies. Any explanation that would convince the Press, the hotel guests, and themselves.

First they tried to find a connection between all the eight people who had hurtled out of the windows. They listed their names, ages, nationalities, professions, room numbers and the dates when they had signed into the hotel. The reasons for their visits, their marital status and what was known of their family background.

On first analysis it appeared that none of them had anything in common. Except the manner of their death. A quick check on the victims' rooms revealed that they had all been dragged from bed: all the bedclothes had been torn off and hurled across the room as though the individuals had been picked up bodily and thrown out by some incredible force.

Edgars suggested that a terrorist group could have entered each room and physically brutalised the victims, though it had been discovered that all the doors but one had been locked from the inside.

'Could each victim have been drugged, then?' Natalie asked.

'Hallucinating? Poisoned?'

They were trying to escape the obvious. The whole hotel had been taken over by a massive psychic manifestation and the sooner they admitted it the better.

She put this to Martineau who, confronted with the idea,

laughed nervously and told her he could in no way present such an idea to the board, let alone the world Press, without some evidence or other.

'What kind of evidence do you want?' she asked.

'Maybe I don't want evidence, Natalie, maybe right now I just want a feasible explanation, a concocted story, perhaps?'

She didn't think twice about what such a deception meant.

She just went back to her office and looked through the list of victims again. Their professions, occupations, hobbies had nothing in common, but what of their beliefs?

Then it came to her. Five of them were Americans, there was one German and a French couple. Supposing they had all been members of a religious sect?

A suicide pact? A sect gone mad, mass hysteria. It had happened in Guyana not that long ago. She would invent a new religion, a new sect, something between the Mormons and Jehovah's Witnesses. A new sect at the point of crisis: a bizarre crisis of faith. She would have to do it secretly, could not do it all alone, she needed help, needed it fast, it would have to be someone she could trust, someone who would understand.

Donald!

She rang immediately, told him she'd be coming over to the flat. Speed was of the essence.

She left the hotel, grabbed a taxi, attempted to relax and calm her nerves, resist the strange excitement at the thought of manufacturing an answer.

The peace in her small flat was unbelievable. Donald made her a welcome cup of tea, sat down next to her and she outlined her idea, begged him to come up with something that would satisfy everyone that such a sect could exist, some sort of evidence that could be produced.

'A medallion?' he suggested. 'A printed card, a symbol of some sort? A book?' But anything too complicated, anything printed would mean bringing in other people.

'A tape?' he said wildly.

'A tape? A recording of some sort, you mean?'

She considered it. Her mind raced with unprecedented enthusiasm.

'My God, Donald, that's brilliant! You've got to help me set it up.'

'To save the hotel's reputation or your sanity?'

'Both. They're interlinked, you know that.'

'Will you be as loyal to me when we're married?'

'More.'

He leaned over and kissed her, then very clearly outlined what he thought they should do.

'First you write out a message that can be whispered into a tape, while I go out and purchase some Sony Walkmans. We tape the message and plant the Walkmans with the recordings in each of the victims' rooms which you then make sure are found by security or the police.

'Will that be enough?'

'We can top it by me disappearing and re-appearing as a witness to the existence of the sect, claiming that I was approached by them, even that one of their members, Cathy, tried to kill me . . . and killed herself.'

'Would you commit yourself and her memory to that?'

'For you, yes.'

'Then let's get going. I think it's superb.'

The moment he left she rang Martineau and told him that she had come up with something which she couldn't explain right then but that she would be back in a couple of hours with the whole story for the media. Tania was to call a Press Conference, he was to stall the police for as long as he could.

She started to imagine how the tape would run, with a little music and just a few words, a few words from the Bible, perhaps fateful words of disaster calling on all followers to kill themselves.

She had a Bible somewhere. She hurriedly looked through a cupboard where she had stored away her old school books and school reports together with old family photograph albums, early drawing books, Latin and French Primers she could never bring herself to throw away.

An old hymn book fell to the floor, and as she picked it up it fell open at a middle page.

Providence? A helping hand from the unknown forces?

It was there, staring her in the face. The Easter Hymn of the Orthodox Church.

Christ is risen from the dead.
He has conquered death with death
And given life to those who were in the tombs.

'Follow him!' she added in a loud whisper. 'Follow him . . . follow him . . . follow him . . .'

Surely that was all that was needed? With some eerie sound effects. Donald could come up with something.

She had a cassette recorder, not a very good one. She talked into it, tried out the first lines of the hymn, played them back. It sounded too much like her, and it would sound too much like him. How else to do it?

The bell rang.

She opened the door, it was Donald carrying a large cardboard box.

'I bought them all at separate shops so as not to raise suspicion. I decided we only needed four, because they work in couples. Have you come up with anything? I thought maybe the Bible . . .'

She read him the lines.

'Yes. Very good. Very good.'

'Have you any suitable music?' she asked.

He went to his pile of records and pulled out a Bartok LP.

'Won't the police think it too much of a coincidence that your own music is similar?'

'It isn't coincidence. It will make credible the idea that the sect wanted me.'

'To write music for them!'

'Why not? And when I refused . . . they cut off my fingers.'

It brought her down to earth. She was enjoying all the deception because it was obliterating the truth of the unknown horrors they had been through. They were manufacturing an excuse for the manifestations for others' sakes, but for their sakes too.

'What if they come here and find you? To ask you questions . . . what will you say?'

‘I won’t be here. I’m going into hiding.’

‘Where?’

‘Far away. I’m not going to tell you.’

They sat down over the recorder and he spoke the hymn’s lines slowly with a two-second interval between each word. He then superimposed the music and on playing it back it sounded amateur but potent enough, and his voice was quite unrecognizable.

They took the four Walkmans and the recorder to the bathroom and, playing the tape they had just made in the bath, recorded it on each individual cassette with a startling hollow effect.

Natalie then took a cab back to the hotel with the four Walkmans in a plastic bag loaded with the cassettes.

It might work.

It might just work.

Meanwhile she blocked off what was at the back of her mind, that though she might allay the fears of future guests and win the praises of the board, the real truth was a mystery still unsolved.

As the taxi came East along Kensington High Street, the traffic snarled up.

‘It’s that bleedin’ hotel,’ the taxi driver said, over his shoulder.

As they approached, she was astonished to see a mass of sightseers who had obviously stopped to look at the scene where unimaginable horror had taken place.

‘Police might not let you in. Staying there are you?’

‘Yes. I’ve been there all week,’ she said calmly.

‘There last night, then?’

‘I slept throughout and wasn’t aware of anything.’

‘Still, eight lunatics did kill themselves, didn’t they?’

‘Religious fanatics,’ she said, ‘it happens.’

The taxi pulled up and she got out and went up the steps, the crowd, well behaved, peered at her as though she were some sort of film star because she had the right to enter, or the nerve, or the money.

‘How are things?’ she asked the doorman as she went in.

‘Merrier,’ he said. ‘Things are getting back to normal. But

you're wanted by the boss.'

She went straight to Martineau.

'Half the directors are suggesting closing the place until it's been discovered what caused the havoc.'

She told him the plan in confidence and he was impressed, giving her the go ahead. They had nothing to lose now, anyway.

She went back to her office, hardly speaking to anyone, told Tania she was going to powder her nose in her room, but instead went to each of the rooms where the fall victims had stayed and, wearing gloves not to leave finger prints, placed a Walkman under each of the mattresses.

She then took off her gloves, returned to her office, cool, calm and collected, to await developments.

After lunch, under Scotland Yard instructions, the Detective Inspector who had been put on the Cathy case came in with a team to make a thorough search of the whole place, particularly the fall victims' rooms, going through every piece of luggage, opening every drawer, every cupboard, lifting the carpets and turning over the mattresses.

They found the Sony Walkmans.

The music was startling, apparently, and the voice strange, and the Inspector quickly put two and two together and swung the enquiry immediately to Carmel Dreihardt and the Genisist sect.

Natalie hadn't expected them to come up with a story that fitted her fantasy to such perfection, nor in such record time, and through Derek Edgars she learned that Dreihardt, far from being a saint, was considered a 'doubtful' character by authorities in the States and certainly not above suspicion for crimes of fraud and misrepresentation. Not that anything had ever been proved.

It was in a meeting with Martineau, when the Inspector made them listen to the Walkman tapes, that she casually said, 'It's the same sort of music that Donald writes.'

'Which Donald would that be, miss?' the Inspector asked, his mind clicking away. 'Not Mr Donald Southam, surely?'

The Inspector followed the lead. The fingers, Cathy's death, Charlie's death.

'Where is Mr Southam?'

No one knew.

And a search was initiated.

The sobriquet THE BLACK HOTEL was first used by the evening paper.

The headline BLACK HOTEL HORROR publicised the disaster, after which everyone, from the national dailies, television, radio, to weekly magazines rang her up.

She was so busy putting up defensive tactics, delaying interviews, issuing denials that everything else worked out extraordinarily easily, as though a sixth sense had intimated that the time was ripe to act.

Natalie was so keyed up by the way the whole business was developing that she had to take a good dose of sleeping pills to get through the night, and the next morning she went back to her office with a somewhat macabre enthusiasm to read through the pile of papers on her desk.

The headlines were startling.

BLACK HOTEL DISASTER.

BLACK HOTEL DEATHS.

BLACK HOTEL MYSTERY MAN VANISHES.

BLACK HOTEL FINGERS FINGERLESS PIANIST.

The company had wanted to put the Palace Plaza on the map, and now it would be engraved on the minds of everyone.

Black Hotel would become household words.

Stories followed about the connection between the suicides and Carmel Dreihardt, her own story, handed out to a reporter off the cuff appeared as an exclusive interview and from experience she knew that that would be the one which would be quoted from now on.

It suggested that a mass suicide pact by an unnamed religious sect had taken place at the Black Hotel and that Donald Southam, Hollywood composer, was hiding somewhere from members of the sect who were after his blood. She had heard of many hotel guests hallucinating, she had in fact slept throughout the so-called ghostly horror which some had said had taken place in the corridors, and had certainly not seen any 'lights'. Everything, she maintained, could be explained logically.

It was not exactly the image she had been told to give the hotel, but at least she was saving the day, and when the papers took it up and she was interviewed for a television diary programme, she was magnificently casual about the whole business. She made sure that the backdrop against which she was interviewed showed the hotel running smoothly.

The rooms where the people had hurled themselves out of the windows were shown, these, she mentioned, would now be used as offices, in case some future guests were superstitious.

When asked whether the management minded the place being called the Black Hotel, she replied, 'Not a bit. Because of its façia it has always been known by the staff and many of our regular guests as the Black Hotel. After all, as someone has said, black is beautiful.'

The police and the press were searching the country nationwide for the 'fingerless pianist', and Natalie settled down to face a mountain of paperwork in her in-tray, letters to be written to the relatives of the deceased, letters to be answered calming nervous future guests.

On the fifth night after the fearful event, when Scotland Yard gave clearance for the use of the rooms, she realized that for at least twenty-four hours she had managed to forget the truth.

She had worked hard at making others forget and she had started to believe her own comforting lies.

The telephone rang, and when she picked up the receiver she heard the recording she and Donald had made together.

It was a brilliant idea ringing her up like that and playing it over the phone. Donald was really imaginative and she held the receiver to Tania's ear with excellent results.

'It's them! The sect! We'd best report it to the police immediately.'

And she allowed Tania to do so.

It was only late that evening, when she got home and sat

down to kick off her shoes in the peace and quiet of her own flat that a feeling of loneliness came over her.

She wanted Donald, needed him, and when an hour or so later the telephone rang and it was him, she realized that if she had ever had any doubts about marrying him, those doubts were now no more.

'How are you?' she asked.

'Fine. All fine. How are things going?'

'Marvellous. Your call to the office this afternoon was brilliant.'

'What call?'

'Playing the recording over the phone. Tania got so excited by it she rang up the police immediately.'

'I made no call,' Donald said, 'I haven't been near a phone all day.'

CHAPTER EIGHT

The cottage that Donald rented was up in the Lake District overlooking Ullswater. It had been a crofter's cottage, extended twice over the years, and was now a holiday let. He had had no difficulty in finding it after a train journey from Euston and he had been in the district before, had even written one of his unsuccessful concertos in a similar house belonging to friends of Cathy's family.

It was Sunday, it was raining, he had no great desire to go out, but he had promised Natalie he would ring her again, so he put on his newly-acquired gum boots, his raincoat and picked out one of the three umbrellas in the stand provided along with all the other things from linen to tea strainer.

It was a lonely place, the nearest other dwelling was about half a mile away – a farmhouse. On his first night he had allowed a fear to overwhelm him, he had lain awake all night. By about seven in the morning he had overcome it and had slept till midday after which he'd managed to put some notes down on paper, a simple composition for two pianos which had been in his head for some time, further inspired when he had looked out on the silver waters of the lake and all the beautiful foliage of the surrounding trees.

The nearest telephone was in the village, outside the sub-post office cum newsagent. He enjoyed the walk there despite the fine drizzle.

He went into the booth and first got all his change ready. It smelt damp and the instrument was old. Since his call of the night before he had decided that Natalie should come and stay with him. She had sounded unnerved, even hysterical, and had not made much sense. He felt that a great deal was going wrong and it was clear she should get right away from the hotel.

He was also in love with her, and wanted to tell her so, and he regretted the physical night they had had together, it had been premature, unromantic and lustful, and not a bit how he felt towards her. He had been fond of Cathy, but Natalie was something different, new and fresh and dramatic. He was not sure that some of the music he had written had not been stimulated by the thought of her, an idyll of her walking in the hills, so romantic that he might well be accused of copying the *Sound of Music*!

He had a simple plan which was to make his whereabouts known to the police, and face the onslaught of the Press, so that he could at least get her out of the hotel himself. Until he had revealed his position they could not meet without endangering the whole story, which was important to her, and so far everything had gone very well. His name had made enough headlines for him to be able to double his fee in the great metropolis of Hollywood, he was sure. Anyone connected with so many deaths and tragedies had to have publicity value. But that was hardly what mattered to him.

As he started dialling Natalie's number the headline of the Sunday newspaper poster outside the sub-post office registered.

BLACK HOTEL COMPOSER IN MOVIE DEAL.

He hung up and went straight into the newsagent to buy the paper.

Natalie's own story occupied the first inside page as an exclusive and he was surprised to read so much about himself.

> As early as April 1980 Donald Southam was approached by a man connected with the Genisists informing him that their religion would help his wife in her blindness. He refused to have anything to do with them. Two years later he discovered that Cathy was privately in contact with the sect. Believing her to be happy he said nothing until a restlessness developed in her shortly after he had been commissioned to compose a piece of music for what he believed to be a choral society. The society turned out to

be the sect and he again refused to have anything to do with them. Cathy, however, begged him to finish the composition. It was this which caused the rift between them. He then deliberately came to play at the Panorama Roof Restaurant to get out of the house, and this was when Cathy tried to assassinate him under the hypnotic influence of the sect. He was then followed throughout the hotel by two men with knives, eventually trapped in the basement refrigerator where they attacked him and severed his fingers – the worst they could do to a musician.

In a special box in the centre of the article his producer was quoted as claiming that a horror film based on the Black Hotel incidents was being scripted and that music by Donald Southam would be used.

He wasn't sure whether to laugh at it all or cry with rage. The whole preposterous business was such a fabrication of lies that he felt he could well lose respect for Natalie for being involved in such total misrepresentation.

But then she had managed to switch the attention of the media and the public from unexplainable horror to glamorous fantasy, and it would be unfair to spoil it.

What he would do, in fact, was bolster it. He would use the system she had set up to get her away from the hotel. He would use those who had used him entirely to his advantage.

He checked his watch. It was eleven, a good time to get Natalie. He patiently listened to all the noises in the receiver once he had dialled her number then eventually she came through, loud and clear.

'What sort of night did you have?'

'Sleepless.'

'I've decided to reveal my whereabouts.'

'Why?'

'So that we can be together sooner. I love you.'

'That's nice, but what do you intend to do, exactly?'

'Marry you and take you to America with me. You've done enough for your hotel, you don't owe them any more loyalty.'

'You're probably right.'

'I love you,' he repeated, 'and want you to be with me.'

'But how are you going to let the authorities know where you are?'

'You're going to do that. You're going to ring up the big time film producer who is using my name to his advantage and you'll tell him I'm staying in Bradford.'

'Where in Bradford?'

'One of the hotels.'

'But which one, Donald?'

'I must leave them a bit of mystery,' he said, 'see you soon, anyway . . .' And he hung up.

He walked slowly back through the drizzle, trying to remember what the papers had said about him . . . MYSTERY OF THE PHANTOM PIANIST . . . HUNT FOR FINGERLESS COMPOSER . . . Neither the police nor the Press had looked too far for him. On the other hand, perhaps he had secluded himself too much. So he would walk into the village now and ask around where he could hire a car to take him to Bradford.

The local pub was deadly; seven earthy farm labourers were drinking their warm beer, and the publican was hardly polite to the stranger in whom they were not a bit interested.

'Anywhere I can hire a car?' he asked.

'Taxi. Old Jack.'

'Where would he be?'

'You can give him a ring from here.'

It took time, but it was arranged. From the moment he got into the back seat of the old Vauxhall he had to listen to old Jack's list of the problems they might encounter on the journey. He'd have to stop for petrol, maybe he'd need oil. He hoped they wouldn't have a puncture. The engine was unlikely to overheat, but you could never tell.

The man irritated him so much that Donald was able to be rude. 'It's only about sixty miles, for God's sake! If you don't mind I haven't slept for several days and need to rest. Just drive me to the biggest hotel in Bradford and wake me up when we're there.'

Jack concentrated on his driving.

Comfortable in the back seat Donald reflected on the fact that before going to America he would never have allowed himself to be driven like this, he would have sat in front with

Jack and chatted. But he'd had the VIP treatment and had enjoyed it. Now he felt dozy and allowed himself to be lulled to sleep.

They stopped at a petrol station but he ignored all the gossip that went on between old Jack and the attendant, and as they drove off again he fell into a heavy sleep to be woken up by an anxious Jack asking him if he was in any kind of trouble.

'Why?'

'We're being followed by two cars.'

Donald looked over his shoulder.

Probably the Press at last.

Maybe the petrol attendant had read his paper, had put two and two together and informed the local journalists. Certainly by the time they got to the Metropole Hotel in Bradford not only were seven reporters and Press cameramen forming a reception committee at the entrance, but two policemen were there as well.

The journalists got to him first.

'Are you Mr Donald Southam?'

'Are you the gentleman that was staying at the Black Hotel?'

'Is it true that you belong to a religious sect?'

'How did you lose the fingers of your right hand?'

He ignored them, made it into reception where a well-dressed man approached him and put out his hand.

'I'm from the film company, sent to look after you.' He was accompanied by two bodyguards of sorts who muscled off the reporters.

They took the lift up to the second floor. Hotel rooms, it seemed, were to be his lot.

'The boss wants to speak to you. I'll get hold of him.'

The line to Los Angeles was beautifully clear, and so was the producer's message. He was to go along with instructions given by the assistant. A lot of money was being gambled on him, a whole film epic. He was not to divulge anything to the Press for as long as possible, he was to handle the police only if it was necessary, he would of course be financially rewarded and a contract was on its way.

Donald listened, hesitated, played hard to get. Others, he

pointed out, were also making wild offers.

'What others?' What wild offers? What do you want? You name it, you can have it!'

'I want to marry Natalie Weir and live in peace ever after,' he said, whimsically.

Silence, then a sigh of relief and laughter.

'The wedding will be the best ever, compliments of yours truly.'

Natalie was in the hairdressing salon when his call came through.

'Where do you want to go on your honeymoon?' Donald asked. 'We're going to have two. One very private one and one courtesy of my film producer.'

'Which one am I allowed to choose?' she asked.

'Both.'

'How about a villa on a remote Greek island for the first? And the second must be in Egypt, with photographs of us kneeling in front of the Sphinx asking for occult wisdom.'

'I'm glad you've got your sense of humour back, but somehow I must curb your flare for publicity,' he said, then told her all that had happened since they had last spoken. 'I'm being driven up to London in some luxury limousine tomorrow morning, so should see you for lunch. Will you be at the hotel?'

'Yes,' she said. 'Will you stay here?'

'Why not? We're going to be married in the chapel, and have the reception there afterwards, so I may as well get used to the idea that I can't separate you from the place.'

'I'm married to my work at the moment, but I do promise to get a divorce,' she said, blew him a kiss and said goodbye.

Martineau took the news philosophically.

He understood. At least he said he understood that she wanted to leave, though he hoped she wasn't getting married just to break away. He had already been approached by the film company about the wedding reception.

'Do you think it'll be safe?' he asked.

'Why shouldn't it be?'

'I have a sneaking feeling,' Martineau said quietly, 'that

maybe your pianist fiancé might have something to do with the disturbances.'

'In what way?' She was astounded to hear that coming from him.

He picked up a sheet of paper and handed it to her. 'Notes I made on a pertinent chapter I was reading in a book on the Occult,' he explained.

> The phenomenon of HAUNTINGS has been known since antiquity, the most often recorded being that of the Poltergeist, a mysterious spirit which creates noises and disturbances (From the German POLTER meaning uproar and GEIST meaning ghost.)
>
> The Poltergeist proves noisy, manifesting itself as the sound of ringing bells, foosteps on wooden floors, the knocking on doors and other familiar house noises. They are usually associated with young children or hypersensitive persons.

'Are you suggesting that Donald is either a child or a hypersensitive person?' Natalie said, handing him back the note.

'Apparently some scientists believe that creative people, who are generally hypersensitive, cause such activities unconsciously. Objects move of their own accord, doors open and close, lights go on and off and the laws of gravity are reversed in their presence.'

'So you believe in the supernatural?' Natalie said, relieved.

'I'm having to. There's no other explanation.'

'And you think Donald may be the unconscious cause?'

'I honestly don't know, but as his wife was a pretty creepy creature; blind, probably psychic and certainly hypersensitive, it's possible that some of it rubbed off on him. Let's just see if we get any more trouble when he returns. Is he coming back soon?'

'Tomorrow. He's coming here for lunch.'

Martineau swivelled his chair right round and stopped to face her again. 'I have to tell you that none of this is going to concern me for much longer. I'm leaving.'

'Of your own accord?'

'The board think I should take a long break, let all this settle down. I'm to take over the Glendale Castle.'

'In the wilds of Scotland? You! What a waste!'

'Oh, you know the mysterious way in which the board thinks.'

The Glendale Castle had the reputation of being a white elephant of a place, and was situated some way north of Aberdeen.

'I can have fun building up the business and showing what I'm made of,' Martineau said, bravely.

'It's only got about twenty rooms.'

'But it's been recently renovated. Besides, I'll be able to play golf.'

'Who's going to take your place here?'

'Tania in your case, a Monsieur Audubon from Geneva in mine. He's also arriving tomorrow, so you'll have to find time in the afternoon away from your loved one to show him around and see that he settles in.'

Monsieur Audubon turned out to be inflexible.

Trained in France and Switzerland, he was a small officious man with no imagination. They had chosen well. He would be ideal for the job. He was not at all interested in the splendour of the hotel, nor the present running of it, only in finding fault. There was dust here, there and everywhere, the tables in the restaurants should be laid out differently – the napkin on the side of the plate not in the glasses – the arrangement of the foyer would have to be changed. The kitchens were not his province but his new chef would see that things were better organized. When Natalie took him up to the bedrooms he told her the beds should be made differently, before going into the bathroom.

'I always try everything. I behave like a client,' he explained, closing the door in her face.

She waited, patiently, not going near the window, not wanting to look out at the magnificent view.

Why was it that some beautiful people died and others who were a pain were spared?

She checked her watch. It was four-thirty, he was being a

long time. Having a bath perhaps? A shower? She hadn't noticed if the towels had been put out, he'd find fault with that anyway.

She checked her watch again. Seven minutes. She'd give him ten.

The next three seemed endless, then she finally moved to the door, listened and on hearing nothing at all, knocked.

No answer.

'Monsieur Audubon?'

Nothing. She tried the door, locked from the inside. She rang security.

When they arrived and opened up, they found him slumped on the floor, having fallen forward from a sitting position on the lavatory. It was not an elegant way to die, but perhaps served him right. Death, to her, had now become so commonplace that she could afford such ungenerous sentiments.

'What did he die of?' she asked Sister, who was called in to examine him.

'Who knows in this place? Heart failure? A seizure due to a fright?'

She wasn't sure she cared any more. It was no longer her responsibility, no longer her hotel. Deaths, ghosts, manifestations, poltergeists, they could have the lot, they were very welcome.

She returned to her office to phone round a few agents to let the cottage, and the flat. From now on Natalie Weir was going to look after Natalie Weir.

On the fourth floor, in the laundry room, Mrs Bream, who was finishing off ironing the trousers for a guest in Room 607, was admiring the beautiful jet black hair of Maureen, the Irish girl who was working for her. Not only did she love that silk black hair, but also the pure whiteness of her skin which she had seen in the restroom when Maureen was undressing and putting on her overall. It had been enough to dream about, and she liked dreaming like that. Now that she had her own staff room in the hotel she could invite girls up to tea, or other things, not that she ever quite had the courage to do it. She wasn't a martinet, but she was strict and the girls liked her for it. Now they were all down in the canteen for the half-hour break before the six o'clock rush to iron the party-goers' clothes.

Maureen was folding up the towels and putting them in neat piles to take down to the various bathrooms first thing in the morning. Mrs Bream watched her as she ironed. She was a beautiful mover too. One of the valets had said that in the disco at the New Year Party she had danced all by herself for hours in front of a mirror, watching her reflection. A right little narcissist that one. Of course she could close the doors and take her into the back linen room and ask her to undress, but she'd find it odd, or maybe not. You could never tell. It had happened the once, back at the Grand. That's how she'd discovered the delights of what another woman could do, which was a lot more than any man could. Her Ernie had been useless, bred pigeons cleverly enough and the two children, just, but otherwise it had been no fun at all.

She spread the white slacks out on the table and was just pressing down the folds between the legs when she saw Maureen lifting up some more towels to put them on top of the pile. It was a silly moment of diversion, but long enough to burn the slacks.

Now she'd never done that before! And as she stared at the terrible brown scorch she noticed that the iron's shape fitted exactly in the crutch of the slacks, like the pattern of pubic hair.

'Oh Maureen, I've just ruined 607's slacks, what am I going to do?'

Maureen came over, wide-eyed and horrified.

'However did you do that, Mrs Bream?'

'Watching you, if you want to know.'

'Watching *me*?'

'You're a beautiful mover and I was just watching you. Look. See how the burn fits exactly in the crutch there, looks like a fanny, doesn't it!'

The girl blushed.

'Well you've got one, haven't you?'

Maureen didn't know where to look.

'Let's see it. Come on. I'll show you mine. I've got lots of curls.'

Mrs Bream put the iron down and grabbed hold of Maureen, who was too startled to move, and started unbuttoning her overall.

She wasn't sure why she was behaving like this, what had got into her, but she held onto Maureen and now tore several of the stubborn buttons off.

'Mrs Bream!' Maureen protested, not daring to hit out, but struggling to free herself.

'Come on! Don't be daft. Take your knickers off!'

Mrs Bream was a big woman, well into her fifties, with big muscles on her. Maureen, frightened now, suddenly stamped on her foot and Mrs Bream's reaction was violent. She lashed out with the back of her hand, caught the young girl on the side of the face with her wrist and sent her flying against the shelves of stacked blankets with such force that the girl, hitting her head, passed out immediately.

Mrs Bream then quite surprisingly and quite illogically picked up Maureen's body and laid it down on the large ironing table, slowly, methodically undressed her, ignoring the blood that was trickling from her nose, lifted her up to a sitting position to take the overall right off and the girl's vest, then let her rest again, admiring the small firm breasts which were now much in evidence. With some delight she tweeked each nipple, then took off the Irish girl's slip, and her shoes, all in one go.

The girl now lay naked like a sacrificial virgin in front of the Goddess Sappho.

For no particular reason, except curiosity, Mrs Bream picked up the hot iron, then pressed it down hard between the girl's legs so that it fitted exactly over thc mass of black curly hair. The skin hissed, the body convulsed in its unconsciousness, there was a fearful smell of burning flesh then Mrs Bream came to her senses, stared down at what she was doing and froze.

She looked at the iron in her hand which was smoking, she looked at the girl on the ironing table and was horrified by what had happened.

Was she mad? Was she possessed?

She turned round to check that nobody else was in the room and saw three old people in the far corner gazing at her, grinning, nodding approval.

Slowly she turned the flat of the heated iron towards herself and placed it against her stomach, easing the point up between her large ample breasts.

It took no time at all for the heat to get through her own overall and the dress underneath. It took no time at all to start burning her own flesh, but she kept it there. She kept it there until she could hear the sizzling, see the smoke and smell the odour of herself being scorched.

There was no pain, only total stupefaction at what she was able to do, and she went on pressing the iron against herself, pressing hard so that she was burning a hole in herself, and she felt the metal of the iron now touching the bones of her rib cage, and she was beginning to bleed, and there was black skin peeling off, and she could no longer see for the smoke and, quite suddenly, such a hideous pain overtook her that she howled.

Several of the laundry girls found her on the floor when they came up from the canteen. Her chest was charred, the red hot iron burning through her bowels, and she was quite dead, like Maureen, naked on the table.

In the kitchens the commis chef, George, was stirring a huge vat of chicken stock. He always made the chicken stock in the afternoon, using all the left-overs from lunch. He was stirring it with a huge wooden ladle and watching young Chris cleaning the stainless steel tables.

He liked young Chris, he particularly liked him when he had taken off his toque. He had nice little golden curls like a girl, and the blue and white check trousers fitted him tightly round his young arse, and the little white jacket, a bum-freezer, showed that off to advantage.

Sixteen, young Chris was, and rumour had it that one of the butchers had had him down in the locker room. So there was half an hour to make a try before the evening roster came on duty. Chris had just started working for him, so was no doubt ambitious as any young sod to get on and please his immediate superior.

'What do you intend specializing in then, Chris?' he asked across the steaming vat.

'Sugar. I want to pull sugar.'

'I want to pull you, son,' he said, laughing.

Young Chris turned round and gave him such a look that he knew there'd be no difficulty. The boy was a dirty little bugger and he wasn't sure he'd quite want those sort of morals in his section of the kitchen, but he'd take advantage of it before getting rid of him.

He stirred the vat once more and wiped his hands down the side of his apron and undid the bow behind.

'Want a feel then?' he said, coming up behind Chris and goosing him.

The boy turned round sharply, holding a knife in his hand. 'No thanks. I'm not like that.'

'Bloody hell! No need to take that attitude, sonny. We're all human you know. You look like a girl, that's all.'

'I've heard about you. I'm not like that.'

'Male chauvinist, are you?'

He didn't mean to, not really, but he brought his knee up between the boy's legs very sharply and Chris doubled up in pain. Just to make sure nothing would come of the incident, he grabbed the boy's wrist, twisted it and forced him to drop the knife.

'Were you going to use that on me then?' he asked, holding him by the throat.

The boy pushed himself forward from the stainless steel table, butting him in the stomach and forcing him back on the greasy floor so that he bumped into one of the hot plates.

His reaction was violent.

'You stupid little tit!' he shouted, and lashed out at him with the back of his clenched fist. It caught Chris across the mouth and sent him flying against the corner of the steel table, then sprawling to the floor, unconscious.

He hadn't realized he was so strong.

George picked up the inert body and, not knowing what

else to do, laid him out on top of the steel table.

The boy had cut his head somewhere at the back and it was bleeding like all head wounds do, but he didn't think it serious. Instead, he found himself undoing the buttons of the little jacket and then unzipping the light cotton checked trousers. There was something there, tucked in among the folds of the briefs and he got it out.

Funny what size sixteen-year-old dicks were, about the same as any other. Then, for no reason at all, he just picked up the boy, carried him to the steaming stock vat and dropped him in, watching the bubbling liquid close over the body.

Seconds later he came out of what felt like a state of drunkenness. He realized what he had been doing and thrust his hands into the fearful boiling mass to get Chris out. As he did so he was aware that someone was watching. He turned and saw three old people standing by the lift doors. They seemed amused by his behaviour, apparently approving of it and, when he looked at his hands in the boiling stock, he could not understand why he felt no heat, no pain. It was so odd that he slowly leaned over and nuzzled his head against Chris's hot greasy stomach. The liquid stock blinded him, the pain was suddenly intense, he reeled back screaming and felt himself slip on the slimy tiles, crash to the floor where he lay, gradually losing consciousness.

At about the same time, in the boiler house, Grant, the Chief Engineer, sitting in his small office with his feet up on the desk, smoking a cigarette and reading the newspaper, casually looked through the windows at his new assistant, Clem, the one of his choosing, who was re-painting some of the pipes, to tell him that for the first time in days the Black Hotel wasn't mentioned.

Though he had felt totally immune from what had gone on upstairs, he did feel a certain pride at being connected with an establishment that was so often in the news, and he was a bit disappointed that Natalie hadn't made the press for once.

She was a strange one, that girl.

As he watched his mate he realized the man was using the wrong colour.

'You stupid git! Look at what you're doing!'

'Oh . . . sorry Grant . . . Sorry, dunno what I was about.'

He had to admit it. He actually regretted asking for this oaf. He wished to God he'd never complained. Bringing in his own staff was the maddest thing he'd ever done, the bloke was thick as four bloody planks.

He wasn't sure why but he was suddenly overwhelmed by an uncontrollable fury, got up and strode down the boiler room gangway, grabbed hold of Clem and his wet paint-brush and painted his face right across the mouth.

'This is green, right? Green's for the electric, right? This is red, right? Red is for the hot steam. Red for hot. Right?'

'Yes Grant, yes . . . It was only that . . .'

He gripped Clem by the throat and with an unexpected surge of strength picked him up bodily and pushed him up against the red pipes that ran from the boiler up to the heating system.

He held him there for a long time, Clem wanting to scream with the agony but unable to because his throat was being squeezed.

Suddenly Clem went quite limp and Grant let go. Clem crumbled to the floor, a bright red weal down the back of his neck.

'Get up, you stupid little bastard!' Grant shouted.

He kicked him gently, but Clem didn't move.

'Silly git!'

He shook Clem's head, but it looked as though the neck was broken, so he picked him up and, on a whim, laid him out on the five parallel pipes that ran from the boiler.

There was a good deal of hissing, the skin on the side of his face blistered immediately. Then Grant realized what he was doing and looked around, terrified, to see if anyone had observed his madness.

There were three guests standing by the office grinning at him. He picked up the live steam hose which went straight up to the kitchens and was used for the quick sterilization of the floor. He disconnected the join, turned it full on and sterilized Clem, holding the jet over his face and watching the skin go puce, the lips crack and the teeth coming through the disintegrating skin.

Then he turned the steam on himself.

It was unbelievably pleasant, like a warm shower, and he put the end in his mouth, drank in the steam, then it suddenly burnt his mouth, his tongue, the back of his throat, the intense hideous heat came up inside his head, through his nose burning the back of his eyeballs – and his heart stopped beating.

Tania, pale, distraught, came into Natalie's office and closed the door behind her.

'What's happened now?'

Tania told her, in a tight whisper, trembling. Mrs Bream, Maureen, the commis chef and his apprentice cook, Grant and Clem in the boiler house.

'When? Exactly when?'

'In the last hour or so.'

She checked her watch.

Donald had arrived at 12.30, they had lunched in the Princes, he had then left for a three o'clock appointment with a music publisher.

It couldn't have anything to do with him.

'I presume Martineau's been informed?'

'Oh yes. His only comment was that we should be thankful it's all been contained within the staff this time. At least only the police need get involved and the hotel can go on being run as though nothing has happened.'

CHAPTER NINE

It was, as Donald's luck would have it, a rather grey day with low cloud base. It reminded him very much of his first wedding which had been a great occasion – for Cathy's parents but not particularly for him.

He had tried unsuccessfully to lie to her on the steps of the Church. After the ceremony he had led her out to the porch and they had both smiled for the photographers and she had whispered, 'What's the weather like?' He had answered, 'White clouds and a blue, blue sky.'

She had tightened her grip on his hand and said, 'You mustn't lie to me, Donald. I have a sixth sense about the weather. It's overcast, rather dull and within an hour it'll rain.'

She had been right.

He had never considered her to be psychic, but there had been an element of the clairvoyant about her. She'd heard things he'd never heard, she'd sensed things he'd never felt. It had been uncanny to begin with but he had got used to it as he had the way she had insisted on arranging the flat with virtually no furniture. It had turned out to be marvellous to have such space to move about in.

Now, like the first time, he was again in a hotel bedroom dressing.

He and Natalie had had a brief rehearsal with the local vicar in the hotel chapel, banked with white flowers, and everything had gone well.

There were several knocks on the door and a series of friends came in to drink champagne and keep him company while the bride dressed fourteen floors below and the moment of commitment came closer.

Then he was left in peace for a while, to enjoy a shower and relax in his white bathrobe standing in front of the large window looking at the panoramic view before there was another knock on the door.

'Come in, it's open!' he shouted.

There was another knock, so he went to open it.

He didn't know them, but they were smiling. Three of them, two men dressed for the wedding in morning suits, the woman in a long mauve dress. They were very old, terribly old, some relations of Natalie, perhaps, whom she had never spoken about.

They came in, not really invited, and he stepped aside politely.

'I'm sorry I'm not dressed, I wasn't expecting . . .'

The woman put up her hand in way of telling him not to worry, then presented her cheek for him to kiss, embracing him.

As she did so he felt very cold, he felt the whole temperature drop, he felt her icy fingers on his wrist and her smile was no longer kind but menacing.

The two men sat down on the sofa, the woman sat in the armchair and they crossed their legs and stared at him.

'Can I offer you anything?' he asked, unsettled.

They shook their ugly heads.

For they were ugly, their skins were grey and they had yellowish sunken eyes. One of the old men seemed to have no teeth at all, the one with the pure white hair. The bald one wore glasses and it was only on studying him a bit longer that Donald suddenly realized he was the same man who had inveigled him into the cold store.

As he froze, aware of the danger, he saw them getting younger. The white head of the man was turning grey, he could actually see the colour changing, gradually becoming darker, and the room was becoming warmer.

The woman was younger too, more attractive, less lined, less pale, her eyes brighter, livelier, and he began to feel more at ease, he suddenly felt that perhaps he could get away.

He smiled, nervously, and crossed the room towards the door pretending he was getting some more champagne. As he did so he realized he wasn't wearing his gloves and immediately changed direction and went into the bedroom to put them on.

It was as he stepped into the bedroom and saw the reflection of the woman in the mirror wearing the same dress and the same jewelry, but now quite young, that he admitted to himself that he was in the presence of the unknown and that he could be in great danger.

All the same he remained outwardly calm and moved over to the dressing-table to pick up a pair of black gloves which he threaded on. When he turned round all three visitors were in the room behind him, all three quite young people, seemingly friendly and well disposed.

'What do you want of me?' he asked, his throat tight.

The woman, who was handsome rather than beautiful, smiled elegantly and by a movement of the hands indicated that she wanted him to take his bathrobe off.

He checked with the two men who were nodding.

Their menace suddenly became sexual, sadistic.

He declined to do what he was bid with a smile, and their smiles became more threatening.

The man with the head of greying hair stepped forward and gently tapped him on the cheek, scolding him, warning him that if he did not do as he was asked, they might harm him.

It was not the tap on the cheek nor the look of aggression that frightened Donald, but the sheer touch of those fingers which were icy cold, and he realized that he had felt them before when they had gripped his hand and torn off his fingers.

What did they intend doing now?

He checked again with the woman who made it clear that she wanted him to remove his bathrobe, holding out her hand to take it from him. She even conveyed by a smile and an expression in her eyes that there was no need to be shy, he was among friends, among people who knew him only too well, among people who had seen him naked before.

He undid the belt, slipped the bathrobe off and handed it to her.

As their hands made contact she pulled him violently to her, both men stepped towards him, he felt himself being picked up bodily, then hurled with immense force against the window.

The blow, as he hit the glass, jarred and hurt him so much that he did not realize the window was shattering and that he was now falling. Then, for a second or two, he had the time to understand exactly what was happening.

She happened to be looking out of the window when it fell past.

The body. Donald's. Her future husband's.

She had no idea what it was of course, but felt a moment of anxiety on seeing the shadow darken the glass.

There was no reason to connect anything falling with Donald, but she did, and held her breath for quite a few seconds in order to overcome the fear. Since the first day of the disasters anything could unsettle her but she had so far managed to keep control.

Some five minutes later there was a knock at the door. She knew the knock, it was that hard, sharp, three tap knock of Martineau's and Martineau had no business coming to her room only a few minutes before she was due to go down with her mother to the chapel.

'There's someone at the door,' her mother said, coming out of the bathroom, adjusting her new hat which matched her navy blue suit. It was the first time her mother had worn a hat in years.

Natalie crossed the room and opened the door.

Martineau and Derek Edgars were in the corridor.

'May we come in?'

She made way for them, introduced them to her mother.

'Something's wrong?'

Martineau nodded gravely.

'Who?' she asked.

She knew who. She already knew who.

It didn't mean just a death, nor the death of her lover, it

meant that the forces were at work again and now seemed to be focusing on *her* life.

'Donald?' she pressed.

He nodded.

Well, she had made it easy for Martineau. She was the typical diplomat, foreseeing the tragedy and nipping embarrassment in the bud for others.

'What's the matter, dear?' her mother asked.

'The wedding's off . . .' she said flatly, then to Martineau, 'I can't tell her. Can you, please?'

She ran past her mother into the bedroom and shut the door.

There were no tears, she couldn't cry, she was stunned that it had now actually happened to someone who mattered to her, someone who was going to take her out of the hell. And she didn't want sympathy, didn't want her mother's comforting words, because they would be meaningless, and she wouldn't be able to explain to her why such a tragedy should have happened.

She came out of the bedroom. Her mother was sitting down with Martineau and Edgars looking at the carpet, bewildered, completely bewildered. She looked up. The question in all their faces in all their eyes was why and what to do?

'It was going to be a small reception, let's just forget it and, if you don't mind, I'll just leave quietly and go home with mother for a few days.'

'I'll have a car waiting for you at staff entrance,' Edgars said, and both men left.

She got her mother's things together without saying a word, put a few more things in her own suitcase already packed for the honeymoon. 'It's best to leave quickly,' she said.

She opened the door for her mother and they walked silently down the corridor and got into the lift.

She pressed the basement button.

She didn't want to see Donald. She had seen the others. It wouldn't help. The glass had shattered. She remembered seeing the pieces falling now, with the shape, the twisting, moving shape, the shape that had been alive at that moment.

She closed her eyes. She wouldn't come back here. She would leave, write a letter of resignation, have her things sent on down to Chichester. She might or might not tell her mother what she believed, right now she just wanted the comfort of her own little bedroom in the cottage, the sound of the birds singing in the trees outside the window, the fields to walk in and a quantity of tranquillizers to make sure she could sleep.

She would never return. She would go and never ever set foot in the hotel again.

The lift stopped.

They were between the ground floor and the lower ground floor.

She pressed the button again, already knowing it would be hopeless.

It wasn't a fault but another manifestation, this time directed against her, she knew that instinctively.

She closed her eyes for a moment hoping to God her mother would not panic. She was a sane quiet woman who usually kept her head in emergencies.

'Not our lucky day . . .' she said, rather in a whisper.

Then the doors opened, slowly, unexpectedly, and instead of facing the blank brick wall which had to be there, both she and her mother found themselves staring at a vast area of rubble and smoking ruins, at a bomb site in the middle of which, not more than six feet away, stood three old people, the white haired man, the bald headed man and the woman, all in evening dress, smiling, grinning knowingly.

Then the doors closed and the lift moved on down, and as she breathed a sigh of relief, she felt her mother slide down beside her, crumbling, her knees giving way in a faint.

The doors opened when they reached the basement, she dragged her out and pressed the alarm.

Outside she could hear the whining of the police cars, the ambulance sirens, the emergency services come to collect Donald.

She laid her mother out on the cement floor, automatically took her pulse, could not find it, looked at her closed eyes, felt for her heart, for her breath.

She had gone very cold. The shock had killed her.

She attended the double funeral at Golders Green Crematorium, with Martineau, Edgars and Tania. It was a quiet affair with no Press who, for once, left her alone with her sadness.

She returned with her friends to the hotel, not knowing what to do or where to go. She did not particularly want to leave, could not face going back down to the cottage in Chichester alone where there would be memories of her mother, nor her own flat where there would be memories of Donald.

Home, once more, seemed therefore to be the London Palace Plaza.

'Unless you have any objections I'd like to stay on at my desk for a week or two. I may not be able to manage much, but if I could help Tania it would take my mind off things,' she told Martineau, who was perfectly agreeable. But when she had put away her things stoically, managing not to think of her new circumstances, the telephone rang and Martineau asked her to come along to the office.

'What would you like to drink? You'll need it,' he said.

'Brandy, then.'

'It's a new directive from the board,' Martineau said. 'They're closing the hotel.'

He hadn't shaved or combed his hair, he wore no tie and his feet were up on the window sill. She had never seen him in such a state.

The directive was simple. A skeleton staff and one PR to remain in the hotel to take care of an examining team coming from America.

'And Scotland's off,' he added.

'Why?'

'You can guess. They want me – and you – to stay on and do the dirty work. We're the only people who know all the facts.'

It took ten days to close the hotel, then the team arrived

from the States. They were hard faced trouble shooters, engineers, electricians, technicians who went through the hotel with a fine tooth comb. They didn't talk much to begin with but eventually gave away the fact that they were assuming that someone, one of their competitors, was trying to discredit the hotel.

They examined all the files, all Natalie's notes, the list of guests, and when she was cross-examined about the whole affair she realized that no way would she ever make these people consider the truth. She let it be, as Martineau suggested.

The place was quiet. She slept at her flat and came in every day, settled down to a sad routine, drinking more than usual to get through the eight hours she was expected to put in.

The American team left, telling Martineau that they were onto something.

For the next three days Natalie did nothing at all but come into the hotel by the staff entrance, say good morning to the cleaners and play cards with Martineau in his office. Then a call came through from the Board.

It was a courtesy call for information only and not to be acted on. The enquiry team had satisfied themselves that the various deaths had been caused by temporarily insane people under the influence of drugs or hypnosis and they were now moving in the direction of Carmel Dreihardt to make a study of his activities. They had concluded that his Sect was at the root of what they termed 'the religious massacres'. The overwhelming proof of this theory was the fact that the manifestations had started very close to the date when Dreihardt and the Genesists had been invited to stay at the hotel.

Natalie was unhappy. Dreihardt had never harmed her, there was no reason for him to be witch hunted. She told Martineau so and he agreed.

'Why don't we go and talk to Krieselman?' he suggested. 'He's a reasonable man who likes you and will listen to you. I think we should go and see him and lay our facts on the table.'

Martineau made an appointment for them to see

Krieselman privately at his Surrey house on the following Sunday afternoon. The weather was good, the drive down pleasant, they were invited to sit on a slightly windy terrace for drinks and Natalie explained what had happened, everything, in chronological order, begging him from the start to hear her through however lunatic it might all sound.

He did as much, attentively, seriously, never once giving signs of disbelief, then ushered them into his study.

It was a large room lined with shelves crowded with books. He pointed to a long line devoted entirely to the occult. 'It's not a subject to which I close my eyes,' he said, 'but you must understand, as I'm sure you do, that the majority of people think it a whole lot of rubbish. Now please sit down and look over at the windows.' He leaned against his large leather topped desk and indicated two comfortable chairs for them to settle in.

'As you see the terrace runs all along the garden side of the house, past three sets of windows. When I bought it, twenty years ago, I was told the place was haunted. I didn't believe it, but one day when I was sitting here I saw a figure pass by the window going from left to right along the terrace. I happened to look up at the clock. It was striking three. Now my wife was in the drawing room which is at the other end of the terrace, there's the hall between, and she saw the figure as well passing from left to right as the clock struck three. We exchanged notes about it, we then saw the figure over the past twenty years seven times in all, always midsummer, always at three, but the remarkable thing was that even if my wife saw the figure at the first stroke of three and I saw it at the third stroke, it meant that it took, at the most, six seconds to cover a distance of twenty yards, which is going some. Yet both of us saw it walking past very slowly, using a walking stick.'

He paused to light a cigarette.

'Enquiries, of course, have told us the story. A shepherd used to tend his sheep on this site where the house was built. One midsummer's day a whole flock had to be slaughtered because of some disease. Nothing exciting. In fact he is not a threatening ghost, simply an anxious one, and I've told you about him to let you know that I believe in the supernatural.'

'So you believe us?'

'Enough to ask you to make your own researches along psychic lines and suggest that maybe you should consider exorcism.'

'Exorcism!' Martineau reacted.

Krieselman crossed the study to a table where all the morning papers were stacked.

'I earmarked this interesting article. A bevy of cardinals and nuns from all over the world are thinking of meeting in London for some form of ecumenical council, I would suggest we invite them to stay at the hotel free. Their mere presence on the premises might frighten away the spirits. It gives you two months to organize and would clear our name for ever if they accepted.' He then pulled out several volumes from the occult shelf and handed them to Natalie.

'Have a read through these. They may or may not help you and, if I were you, I'd try and find out who the three old people were.'

She invited Madame Raymonda to come and stay one night at the hotel for a generous fee, and the clairvoyant arrived bringing her cat, whom she claimed was psychic.

'If there are still presences in the place my dear, he'll feel them out.'

Together, after dark, they walked the corridors of every floor of the hotel, opening doors and going into rooms at random, standing silently in every suite that had seen a death, and Natalie primed herself with sufficient vodka to see the exercise through, though afterwards she felt exhausted and drained, specially as they met up with nothing at all unusual.

She repeated the experiment with two other mediums, one man and one woman, both of whom declared that there was no sign whatsoever of any presences and charged a hundred guineas each for saying so. At least all three clairvoyants agreed.

So what could it be?

She decided to concentrate on the six staff who had died so

horribly and started to investigate the family background of each individual separately. Somewhere there had to be a reason.

She set herself the task of seeing one relative every day. On some days she managed to visit two. Mrs Bream's home was the nearest, Maureen's the farthest, in Dublin. Very soon one small connection emerged. Of the six, each had received assurances from Monsieur Audubon that they would not only be employed by him in the hotel, but promoted. All had worked for Monsieur Audubon before, or knew him. Mrs Bream had been with him at the Grand Hotel, Eastbourne, Maureen had worked for him privately as a maid, George the Chef had been in Geneva with him for a year and the lad, Christopher, was Audubon's nephew by marriage. Grant had worked at the Grand and so had Clem, so that one way or another there was a link, and it was a link she was looking for.

Researching Audubon's history she could come up with nothing significant except that he had died at the same time on the same day as the others.

For a while she worked on the sect theory, invented by her but which, by some incredible coincidence, might have hit the nail on the head. Was it possible for a group of people to be so powerful and so well organized that they could somehow have manufactured the ghosts? The last time she had seen them, with her mother in the lift, a whole film set would have had to be constructed to create the illusion of a desolate bomb site, unless she herself had been hallucinating under the influence of a drug.

She put that problem to Martineau and he suggested that she should come and spend a week-end with him and his wife at their country cottage in Wiltshire, where they would be able to talk in the peace and quiet of unhaunted surroundings.

She gladly accepted.

The cottage was pleasant, though not as luxurious or as well furnished as she had expected. David Martineau at home was quite different to the strict, neat executive he pretended to be at the hotel.

By the fireside after dinner, Martineau was sitting deep down in the comfort of a cosy armchair, and Charmion, his wife, was sitting on the floor by his side with the dog. The children were up in bed.

Charmion, who was reading through all the reports on the hauntings, looked up and smiled pleasantly at Natalie. 'May I ask you a very personal question?'

'Yes, of course.'

'It is embarrassing but I think it important. Did you ever sleep with any of the men who died?'

She'd slept with four of them, she knew that straight away. It was something that had occurred to her, and she took so long in answering that Charmion helped her in her hesitation.

'How many of them?'

'Four.' Natalie said, looking up.

Martineau was the one to react, surprised, nearly hurt it seemed.

'Can you name them?'

'Felix Pearsall, the journalist, Robert Clariss from Paris, Donald Southam and . . . Grant the Chief Engineer.'

'Grant?' Martineau was astonished.

'I wouldn't have done unless I'd wanted to.'

'But he's . . .'

'Common? A bit of rough I think they call it.' She was very amused by Martineau's jealous reaction, till she realized that Charmion had gauged it as such as well.

'Because you employ her doesn't mean to say you own her, body and soul, David,' she said.

'No . . . no of course not. But Grant!'

'Anyway I did. Why?' Natalie said, turning to Charmion.

'Do you think there's any connection?'

'Not unless I'm some sort of witch. There is, of course, one way of finding out.'

'What?' It was Martineau, being curious.

'I should sleep with someone else and see if they survive the experience!'

She said it lightly, jokingly, but deep down she wasn't sure that that wasn't exactly what she was going to do. She needed some diversion now, she needed to be active in finding out what it was all about. She was plagued by the ghosts, living the ghosts, she had to do something.

She also realized that in one quick confession she had lost her boss's respect.

Well, if he was a bed snob that was his problem. She hardly cared anymore. She was too tired, too exhausted. She realized that telling him had been one of those instant mistakes which are never forgiven let alone forgotten.

Then Charmion asked another question which was much more pertinent. Though the various reports pinpointed the manifestations as having started when Carmel Dreihardt had first been invited to the hotel, was it not also about the time when Natalie herself had started working there? Natalie was the one who saw the ghosts, the manifestations always occurred when she was in the hotel, and they also occurred on the occasions when she had considered leaving her job.

How often had she truly decided to leave?

Four times?

Did those dates coincide with the manifestations?

It was such an intriguing idea that both she and Martineau agree that they should go back to London immediately to check their various diaries.

They drove on the empty night roads in silence. Natalie felt a definite coldness from Martineau because of her confession. She put the silence to good use by dropping off to sleep in a cosy slumber.

When they got to London and the hotel, they went in by the staff entrance and made their way up the back stairs to the main foyer which in its emptiness was eerie, spooky and not a bit welcoming.

They went to their respective offices, Natalie joining Martineau once she had collected her diary. A quick glance at the days when she had marked a black asterisk because of the visions confirmed that there was a connection. Though she had never actually written 'Am thinking of leaving', Robert Clariss's offer of New York, and Donald's marriage proposal were memorable occasions.

But why? Why?

What had she got to do with three people and a new hotel?

She sat down and thought through all her researches. What connection could she possibly have, and why would the ghosts manifest themselves when she was threatening to leave?

Threatening to leave?

Did they for some reason want her there? Her? If it was that simple, then she would stay.

'I'm staying!' she said out loud. 'I'm staying in this hotel for at least another year, and I will stay longer if you promise to behave.'

She said it standing up, facing the door, then she turned to look at Martineau who for a moment was a trifle scared of her. He smiled painfully, anxiously.

'If they want me here, I'll stay here,' she repeated, 'I'll make a bargain with them that I will not leave, but I must find out why they are interested in me.'

Martineau now stood up and, a little embarrassed, also addressed the door.

'As manager of this hotel I solemnly promise to employ Natalie Weir permanently if it is so desired, on the one understanding that she will be sacked, fired, and kicked out following the very next sign of a supernatural occurrence.'

He sat down again, and had to take out his handkerchief to mop his brow. 'I've never felt so stupid and yet so sincere,' he said.

'You realize that if they do cause an incident and you do fire me, you may very well be disposed of by them?' Natalie said.

'They can dispose of me now if they so wish. But if there is a grain of truth in all that we are assuming, albeit a little childishly and naively, then they will know, by instinct one hopes, that both of us have had enough and will do anything to get the hotel re-opened again.'

He got up and went to the cocktail cabinet, pouring out two good glasses of whisky.

'And I'll tell you this much, Natalie, if nothing happens for a year and everything runs smoothly, I'll suggest you are granted a permanent room here, whether you work for us or not. I, of course, may not go on as manager. Between you and me, it's all been a bit too much and I may well resign.'

He stopped on his way back to the cocktail cabinet, bottle in hand, as though waiting to be struck by lightening. Then smiled and carried on.

'It's quite a relief knowing that you're the scapegoat, Natalie.'

CHAPTER TEN

Two peaceful months passed.

A trickle of staff returned to the hotel, then a few privileged guests at reduced prices, then the whole hotel was opened for Krieselman's ecumenical bonanza.

On the appointed day a stream of cars drew up outside the hotel unloading three hundred nuns and priests, monks and cardinals.

Natalie had arranged for ecclesiastical music to be piped through the system, the Suzerain Suite was converted into the nun's refectory, the Monarch Suite into the priests' and monks'. The bars were closed, the staff told to keep their voices lower than usual, the whole atmosphere was to be subdued but despite all this the cardinals and priests and monks and nuns managed to be very jolly. The senior dignitaries were given the fifth floor, the nuns the seventh and eighth, the remaining priests and monks the tenth, eleventh and twelfth.

Natalie was surprised at how much they spent and how much wine was consumed. They insisted on the best. Some of the nuns were exceedingly pretty and they all came from so many different countries that the high pitch of conversation as they tried to communicate could only be described as a continual din. It was also a colourful pageant for with their various ranks and various orders, they wore capes, hats, birettas, hoods, vestments and canonical robes. On watching the first assembly from the top of the stairs overlooking the foyer she had the impression that the renaissance had invaded the twentieth century.

Tania came back, and so did some of the staff, some

looking really well and tanned after a long holiday. Others were rather anxious that the place might still be plagued by the Genisists, though the Catholic army helped to dispel this.

Every day Natalie went to the small chapel and made herself pray with the nuns, partly because it was good PR policy and partly because she felt that begging for peace might actually work. She also watched for any signs of the terrible three.

On the nun's floor one day she thought that something was about to happen, but then realized that the unsettling atmosphere was caused by the strange way the nuns floated down the corridor with their robes flapping lightly behind them, their rosaries clicking in the ecclesiastical silence.

On the fourth night, unable to sleep despite tranquillisers, aware that she was very much on edge with only two more days to go and a clear record so far, she went up to the eighth floor to Donald's old room, looking, she realized, for trouble, but wanting to confront the ghosts herself if they were ever to appear.

As she walked down the silent corridor, at two in the morning, she felt strangely at home in the darkness, comfortable, happy even, a feeling of elation and security.

Could it all be over?

Then she heard a sound, a chilling whisper followed by a titter from one of the unoccupied rooms.

Did she have the courage?

Had she not come up for this very reason, to seek and find, to confront.

Or had she been drawn?

She approached the room. Number 816.

It had no connection with anything that had happened in the past.

Silently she inserted the pass-key and eased the door of the suite open.

A table lamp was on in the sitting room and the bedroom door was ajar. From beyond it came a rustling sound.

She crossed over silently.

There were two of them, a man and a woman, naked on the double bed making passionate love. On the floor was a monk's habit, on a chair a nun's robes. She had read of such unions in Boccaccio's *Decameron*.

She smiled apologetically and closed the door, but the monk was after her immediately, covering his erection with one hand, then hiding behind the half open door and talking to her through the crack as though he were in a confessional.

'Plees, plees, to say nothing to no one . . .'

'I am discretion itself,' she said. 'Have no fear.' And she made the sign of the cross.

The incident amused her, made her happy in a way, the thought that physical pleasure was not entirely denied them. The nun had been extremely beautiful, even if the monk had looked a little wild and extremely hairy.

She took the lift down.

Was sex so sinful? Had they been motivated by an evil force to go against their doctrines? Were all the monks sleeping with all the nuns, the whole hotel a sacrilegious brothel?

But whether from their holiness, or their sacrilegiousness, the remainder of their conference passed off without incident.

It took time, a further three months, before everything returned to absolute normal. The low-key but good publicity gained by having the ecclesiastics in the hotel helped clear its black name, the Holy Hotel one newspaper dubbed it, but that didn't stick.

She genuinely felt more secure however, content even, and it was rewarding to see the hotel gradually picking up business and the foyer full of guests coming and going again.

She organized exhibitions, conferences, adopted the policy of keeping the hotel out of the news for as long as possible, giving time for everyone to forget the bad image.

Martineau himself seemed to forget her indiscretion with Grant, forgave the lapse, was kind to her, affectionate, though always careful not to cross the line into intimacy.

Was he frightened of her, deep down?

Had Charmion's suggestion that sleeping with her was tantamount to suicide put him off for ever?

The idea intrigued her and worried her too and one evening, up in the Panorama Bar, a warm night, sultry, she admitted to herself that after too much time without a man, she could surely allow herself a little indulgence.

Besides, she would have to find out sooner or later whether she was a killer, and best, surely, to do it with a stranger.

Nikos happened to be standing by the restaurant door as these thoughts crossed her mind. Nikos the Greek, Nikos the beautiful, twenty, twenty-two perhaps, black curly hair with the face of a young god.

Why not, one day when her frustration really became unbearable?

Which it did, the following afternoon.

'Well Mr Greek God, now is your chance,' she thought to herself as she made her way to the Princes' Restaurant just after lunch for the specific purpose of having another look at him.

The Princes was always pleasing, for some reason. It had a cosy atmosphere about it that the other two restaurants didn't have, maybe because of its coral coloured carpet and curtains, or the low ceiling, or again its coolness on a hot summer's day.

She went in through the swing doors and spotted him immediately. He was fooling around as usual with the other young waiters, but on seeing her stopped, arched his eyebrows and blew her a cheeky kiss, nudging his colleagues.

'All right Nikos, for about two months now you've been blowing me kisses. What do you want of me?'

He drew her away from his colleagues, who scattered discreetly. 'You are so beautiful, so attractive, that I cannot help myself.'

'Fantastic, thank you for the compliment. How long will it go on for?'

'For until you give me a chance to prove to you how much I love you.'

'Explain yourself, I don't understand,' she said, deliberately being awkward.

'I want to make love to you. I am very good lover.'

'You are? Who says so?'

'All the women I have made love to.'

'How many's that?'

'Enough to have confidence when a woman is in my arms.'

'Practice makes perfect?'

'Perfect,' he repeated, smiling.

She had to admit he excited her, his lips were very sexy.

So why shouldn't she have herself a young Greek waiter, just the once. She hoped to God she wouldn't grow too fond of him, that was all. How awful to be in the emotional clutches of such a boy.

'Know the number of my room?' she asked blatantly.

'209.'

She was surprised.

'See you when you come off duty tonight then,' she said.

He was so grateful, so pleased, because he'd be able to boast about the conquest to come or because she actually attracted him? He certainly attracted her. And he had been so definite and clear about it. With anyone else of that age it would have been blushes and nudges, but no, it had all been handled very coolly.

For the rest of the day she thought of little else and as evening wore on and midnight approached she became more and more excited at the prospect of seeing him. She dressed carefully, making sure he wouldn't have anything to criticize. His damned conceit and talk of other women had worked on her, she was competing with all the 'other' girls, was determined to better them.

It was ridiculous!

There was a soft knock on the door.

As she opened it, the thought crossed her mind that she might be flirting with disaster. If Charmion's suggestion had been correct, was she not simply offering this young man up as a sacrifice to the ghosts?

She opened the door and was astonished at the effort he had made.

She had never seen him in anything but his waiter's uniform, now he was standing there in a light beige suit, a pale blue shirt and tie, beige canvas shoes, his hair washed and mop combed. He was holding a single rose.

She had to hand it to him, he knew how to dazzle.

'Come in,' she said. She was pleased she had bothered to dress a little. She had simply put on a loose cocktail dress and had put a bottle of white wine on ice, but he would pick up on what it meant.

She took the rose, kissed it, kissed him lightly on the cheek as though he had been an old friend, and suggested he should sit down.

That was the moment when he gave his nervousness away.

He looked around the room trying to find something he could admire but realized it was all hotel junk, so he was unable to say anything complimentary, which unsettled him.

He sat down on the sofa and crossed his legs, being careful about the creases in his trousers.

Sitting in the luxurious surroundings in which he worked threw him. He was out of his depth now and that was where she would hold him for a while if she could.

She imagined him, of course, diving off some rocks in Corfu, wearing a very small slip, his dark tan competing with her blotchy sunburnt skin. Here she was her own sophisticated self and he was a waiter, in disguise, but still a waiter.

Uncomfortable, he uncrossed his legs and leaned forward to rest his elbows on his knees, unable to think of anything to say.

'Wine?' she offered.

'Please.'

'Where did you learn your English?'

'In Athens. In the university.'

'You didn't go to university, Nikos. I know all about you, so don't try to impress me.'

'The university of life,' he corrected quickly.

It was good. She liked it enough.

'I know more about you than you know about me,' she said. 'I looked you up in the files.'

'It's all lies, the file. I am really the son of a millionaire ship owner doing an apprenticeship here in London before taking over the chain of hotels run by my father.'

'Not bad. Not true, but not bad.'

She poured out two glasses of wine, handed him one and sat down next to him. He sipped it before she did, realized he should have waited for her, that she might think it rude, and apologized with a beautiful smile.

His youth actually made her feel old, she realized, he was also very slightly smaller than her, which didn't help. She would go through with it, but at twenty-five, she really didn't need to dial a gigolo.

All the same she reached out for a little curl behind his right ear and played with it.

'I know about you also,' he said.

'Tell me.'

'You are a very powerful woman, probably the most powerful in this hotel chain, much more than Martinet, and you control everything in this hotel. You are brilliant with the Press but are having a very hard time with this sect who are trying to take over.'

It was what the staff said of her, she knew that, nothing new. 'Good,' she said, 'but how old am I?'

'Twenty-five.'

'That's very accurate.'

'I have had you looked up in the files too,' he said proudly.

'Who by?'

'That would be telling.'

'Tania?' she suggested.

He shrugged his shoulders.

She had never thought of Tania sleeping around.

But why not?

And she realized he was studying her, aware no doubt that the thought of him and Tania together had upset her.

He reached out and caressed her cheek with the back of his fingers.

He did it gently, pleasantly. She could not object. He then took her hand from where it was resting behind him on the back of the sofa and kissed it, first the fingers, then planting his lips in the palm.

'You have very beautiful hands,' he said.

'Thank you.'

He was winning now. He had passed through the critical barrier and had cleverly moved her onto his own territory. She watched as he gently kissed each of her finger-tips.

Somehow he moved very swiftly across the sofa so that he was partly on his knees yet in a perfectly comfortable position to kiss her on the mouth, which he did.

That she liked, admired. Compared to poor Donald, he was so confident, so commanding. If she had ever hesitated to get involved in a casual relationship it had been because of the awkwardness of most men with the opening gambits. The fact that she so often had had to make the man feel at ease.

With Nikos there was no question of that, he was making her feel wanted. That was what he was doing, he was making her feel wanted, making her feel that she was going to give him pleasure.

He gently removed the glass from her hand and took her in his arms, all sitting and kneeling down, all without fumbling or being in any way gauche. He embraced her so passionately that she actually felt herself trembling. Her! Trembling at the touch of a young man!

He did not, as she expected, now place his hands on her breasts, or down between her legs, but kept on kissing her simply on the lips and everywhere above the neck line.

The boy was a genius and she would soon have to believe in everything that had been said about the Greeks as lovers.

He disengaged himself, stood up, never let go of her finger-tips, then somehow lifted her up from the sofa so that they were standing. He picked her up bodily, gently, and took her to the bedroom where he managed to undo the three buttons of her dress and the belt without her being aware of what he was doing before laying her down on the bed itself.

He then sat down beside her and took off her shoes.

At no time was there any suggestion that she should do anything but allow him to take care of her. She was not to take off any of her clothes, let alone his, that was his duty, his pleasure. First one shoe, a kiss on the foot, on the ankle. The other shoe, the same procedure. She had not drunk enough to be immune to the fact that this was a routine which he had probably followed countless times with others, but she didn't mind. It was like observing a professional lover, whatever they were.

Now he moved up and kissed her on the lips again, gently as always, at the same time removing the dress which was already undone.

He kissed her all the time so that she never felt naked and soon found herself topless, with just her slip, nothing else.

He now lowered the lights with the dimmer switch, knowing exactly where to find it, and in the semi-darkness he very quickly and expertly stripped. His jacket, his shoes, the same time, his socks, next his shirt. Suddenly he stood with his suntanned torso contrasting with the well creased beige trousers. He unzipped and, of course, he wore no briefs at all. He was there, semi-erect.

She did not move at all but stared at him, at it, her arms crossed over her breasts, demurely.

Looking at her all the while, like a little boy playing at doctors and nurses, he very delicately removed her slip, kissed her navel and moved down.

She could not, in all honesty, say that it was any different to any other similar experience, but the lead up had excited her and therefore he was ahead on points.

He moved well, making a lot of unnecessary noises, passionate hums and groans, kissing her continually, and at one moment took both her hands placing them on his buttocks, wanting her to hold him tightly there.

It was good, pleasant, but her mind was wandering very far off. To Donald, to Robert Clariss, to Martineau, who would not approve. She closed her eyes as he hit a tender spot, a very tender spot indeed and it was so good that she begged him not to stop, begged God that he would not suddenly explode inside her and drift off into some sleep of his own beside her.

The climax was coming. While that peak lasted she was still able to be elsewhere and she was enjoying it all, her eyes firmly closed, listening to his moans, her own murmurs, the bed springs. Then, as it came very close, she opened her eyes and found herself staring at a strange elderly round face, puce, swollen with the effort, Carmel Dreihardt's face, his white hair falling down over his forehead, beads of sweat pouring down his temples. The image did not last long but long enough for her to see the whole of him, the flabby whiteness of his chest and arms, the frown, the grimacing pain as his energy was being sapped.

She gasped, wanted to scream and push him away, but he

came, and she closed her eyes at the feel of the fusion, the warm flood. It was a moment of delicious disgust and when she opened her eyes again she saw the pleasing young Nikos looking at her, watching her, still working himself into her determined that she should have every drop of his enjoyment.

'Are you all right?' he asked.

'Oh yes . . . yes. Thank you,' she said.

Then he allowed himself to collapse on top of her, pull out and roll over to lie exhausted beside her, panting, smiling at his victory.

'You looked quite frightened for a moment,' he said, proudly amused.

'Perhaps you were frightening?'

So, she thought as she relaxed, she'd had herself a waiter. She didn't care a damn what anyone thought of her, either among the staff or the management or the board.

She knew what she cared about, what she was frightened of.

Carmel Dreihardt. The ghost? Taking over Nikos's body. A manifestation produced by the sex act? How?

Was it imagination or some form of unbelievable hypnosis?

It was more down to earth, less fearful than anything emanating from dead spirits, the idea of the evangelist being behind it all. A magician producing fantasies in people's minds to cause chaos, in order to control.

She sighed deeply, realizing that this new theory was a relief, thankful that the three old people might only be an image created by a living being, terrifying, demonic, evil, but at least of this world.

And Nikos, mistaking the sigh for contentment, sweetly squeezed her hand. What she didn't want now, of course, was for anything to happen to him.

She was woken up by the telephone ringing at a quarter past eight. She stretched across Nikos's smooth tanned shoulder blades and reached for the receiver.

'Hallo . . .?'

'It's Martineau. Are you alone?'

'That's an indiscreet question, and a rude one.'

'I'm sorry, but I must see you immediately. A matter of urgency.'

'I'll be with you. Give me a few minutes.'

She got up and dressed quickly in her usual morning outfit, brushed her teeth, combed her hair, wiped off her make-up and just put a touch of colour where it was necessary.

At the door she looked back at Nikos who had not moved at all and blew him a romantic kiss.

As she walked down the corridor to Martineau's office she felt confident that she looked good and in no way would seem as depraved as she felt.

She knocked on the door and went in.

'I've just heard from the great research team in the States,' he said, from behind his desk. 'Carmel Dreihardt is totally in the clear. He has been most helpful, they found him in some hide-out of a house in the wilds of Vermont, alone with his family writing a book. There is not one shred of evidence that he could ever have been connected with a religious sect or cult who would cause us such problems and he let anyone who wished to examine all his diaries and accounts.'

She was back to square one.

'The board think the news very significant and want plenty of publicity about it. They think that by clearing Dreihardt's name of malpractice it will clear the name of the hotel. I personally disagree because it just poses the question of who *is* responsible. They prefer, however, to think in terms of terrorist activities.'

'I'll work on it,' Natalie mumbled. 'I'll get something out this morning.'

She left Martineau and returned to her room. Terrorism was understandable to everyone, that was why they wanted to lean that way. She wasn't sure she cared anymore anyway.

Nikos was still fast asleep, had not moved an inch.

He had not moved.

She approached the bed, his side, to look at his face without disturbing him. He was pale. God he was pale. She touched his cheek. It was cold. She pulled back the sheet a little, found one of his wrists and tried to feel the pulse, then placed her hand on his chest.

Nothing. No heart beat. No life.

She closed her eyes, forced herself to think back at the moment when she had seen Dreihardt breathing over her.

It had not been Dreihardt then. Only her imagination. Or one of the three, the old man with the white hair?

She would have to leave. She would have to leave the hotel now and forever of her own accord.

She didn't understand why, but somehow *she* was responsible for the psychic activity. If there was need for a hypersensitive person to cause the manifestation, then, apparently, it was she.

It was time to run for it.

She opened the door, stepped out into the corridor and felt the whole building vibrate.

The main stairs, which had received particular attention and praise from the critics in architectural magazines when the hotel opened, ran the whole height of the hotel. They were extremely wide and carpeted from top to bottom, the walls were lined with black glass, the balustrades of black glass panels and ornamental brass rails.

As she ran down, the glass on the walls started to shatter. Like forked lightning, the panels cracked in darting lines that followed her.

She stopped, the shattering stopped, she went on down, the panels split again.

As she raced on down she became aware of the people on the landings. There was a hum in the air, a constant drumming sound that reverberated and shook the very foundations.

On reaching the first floor, where the landing opened out into a hall leading to the banqueting rooms and suites, Natalie saw that the chandeliers were swinging, not gently, but violently, the crystal droplets were tinkling like agitated bells. It was so much like an overdramatized scene in a horror movie, so much the sum and substance of deliberately manufactured fear, that it gave her a second wind and enabled her to stop, stand still for a moment and watch the unbelievable scene developing.

The three heavy chandeliers were jumping on their chains, and there was humour in the movement.

The spirits, whatever was possessing the hotel, were at work again.

A small crowd of guests were gathered round the Monarch Suite doors where an exhibition of oriental fabrics had finished and been cleared that day. The room, a vast area covered with a beautiful light beige and brown carpet, was the pride of the hotel.

She approached to see what was happening and as she looked in the whole wall to wall carpet, its massive width and length, was like a sea. The heavy pile was being lifted and shaken like waves in a force ten gale and the noise in the room was as though a thousand people were hissing through clenched teeth.

Then there was a roar behind them, a shattering boom of an explosion and the doors of the Princes' Restaurant burst open and every possible object was hurled out in a cascade of crockery, glass and cutlery, table cloths, tables and chairs, ash trays, lamps, trolleys, were propelled out as though caught in the path of an uncontrollable jet stream, and those who got in the way were cut to ribbons.

Now the manifestations let loose their violence.

As though the force was moving upwards through the hotel the first to be affected was Grant's replacement, the new Chief Engineer who was in the basement boiler house. He became aware of a strange ticking sound. It sounded just like a time bomb. Though he had never actually heard one, he had watched enough bomb disposal units on television doing their heroics to know what they were supposed to sound like. But then the ticking was not constant, and it became louder. He stood up, trying to discern where the sound was actually coming from and as he stepped out of his office he realized that it came from all the pipes, which made no sense at all. He checked the various gauges and dials, all was normal. The ticking now seemed to be moving along the blue cold conduits, then along the green electric cables, round the boilers, inside the yellow oil pipeline, a ticking so loud that he had to block his ears. As it dawned on him that something really fearful might be happening, an earthquake perhaps, he started for the emergency exit and just as he reached it, the ticking stopped.

On the next floor up the morning roster of chefs cooking breakfast were startled when all the oven and refrigerator doors suddenly flew open and food hurtled out, to be smacked hard against the white tiled walls as though some invisible and very temperamental giants were having a bun fight.

In the surgery, on the second floor, Sister, who had just administered to a guest who had a painful blocked ear, was writing out her report on the patient when she heard a crash behind her and turned to see the glass case of sterilized surgical instruments hover a foot or so above the floor, tilt, the locked doors open, and the contents spill out. A pair of scissors and a scalpel floating dangerously close to her before being dropped in the waste paper basket.

On the third floor all the doors of the individual bedrooms were automatically locked, imprisoning the occupants who were trying to get out because their rooms reverberated with a high pitched whine which was becoming painful in its intensity.

On the fourth floor, the delicate Japanese wall paper was peeled off in strips in twenty-eight rooms at the same time. On the fifth, in all twenty-eight private bathrooms the mirrors above the washbasins were suddenly struck, dead centre, by a force that fractured the glass in a cobweb pattern. On the sixth the carpets in the corridors were ripped up and shaken. On the seventh the ceiling plaster in every room cracked and fell like snowflakes. From the eighth to the twelfth floor everything electrical was switched on and off, elevators jammed while the rhythmic buzzing of electric shavers, hair dryers, heaters, refrigerators, and the air conditioning system played havoc with the nerves. From the thirteenth to the seventeenth a fearful silence blanketed everything and an oppressive darkness, an intangible void, gripped every individual who walked down the corridors trying to find out what was happening.

In room 1810 on the eighteenth floor a young honeymoon couple who were making love were dragged off the bed by their feet, naked into the corridor, while in room 1820 a commis chef who had secretly paid a visit to one of the room service maids felt himself being held upside down by his feet and shaken violently for several seconds before being dropped unceremoniously on top of her.

In the Panorama Restaurant, where all was silent, the lid of the piano was slowly lifted and an invisible finger played a simple tune, before the lid was closed again.

Then there was silence.

Complete silence throughout the hotel.

The people, stunned, did not move for quite a while not understanding what could have been happening, incapable of finding any logical explanations to pacify their terror. Natalie moved with others towards the exit doors but as it became clear that the horrors had stopped, she started to walk more and more quickly against the mainstream of stupefied guests, towards Martineau's office.

There was such chaos everywhere that it was pointless trying to help people sort themselves out. No one seemed to know why they were where they were, and everyone was looking for someone in authority.

She reached the office and went in through a small crowd of clerics who were waiting for explanations. She rudely shut the door in their faces, locked it and turned to face her boss.

'First let's see if this works,' he said, picking up the phone.

It did.

'OK. Now we ring through to all the staff to meet us in the staff restaurant. You get hold of all the heads and tell them to round up all their sections. I'll do the catering, you do the services.'

They sat down, each at a house phone, and started dialling.

It took half an hour to get them all together. They ignored the guests knowing that calm and efficiency would only be restored if the staff were told exactly what to do.

When everyone was assembled, Martineau got up on a table and addressed them much as a commanding officer might his troops before battle.

'Don't ask questions, I don't know at this moment in time, any more what has been happening than you do. It's morning, all is going to be all right. Just go to your various stations immediately and report back to me what the state of your section is. Then if we can get one breakfast room ready we will deal with the guests.'

They were well disciplined, the nickname Martinet Martineau was appropriate, after all.

The telephone started buzzing in his office and it was like being on the bridge of an ocean liner that had been attacked and was sinking.

Princes Restaurant was out of action. Monarch Suite out of action. Panorama Restaurant untouched. Queen's Restaurant normal. Kitchen on first floor normal. Basement kitchens disastcr area.

The outside cleaning staff who arrived for normal work at six were confused: the police keeping them waiting, then they were let in and told to work systematically from the main service floor up.

Of the four hundred and twenty-five rooms, forty-three were vacant. It was a matter of shifting guests from the worst hit to the clean ones with the minimum of fuss.

A list was made of those guests who wished to complain, of those who wished to leave immediately and have their possessions sent on to another hotel, of those who wanted to claim damages. After three hours of incessant work the hotel began to regain a sense of normality.

Then the outside phones started ringing; the media in full force determined to get the horror story to end all horror stories.

She denied everything, but they had already got hold of witnesses and by the late television news the hotel was again the lead feature glueing the viewer to his set with the fearful accounts of what had happened, and close up interviews of harassed guests recounting what they had seen, what they had heard, what they had experienced.

The next morning the breakfast tables were assaulted with more damning headlines.

BLACK MAUSOLEUM TERROR.

BLACK HOTEL HELL HORROR.

BLACK HOTEL – BLACK DEATH.

CHAPTER ELEVEN

Martineau had a drink ready for her. He indicated that she should sit down and make herself comfortable, again.

'I've had another directive from the board.'

'Tell,' she said.

'We're closing for good.'

How could she be surprised. 'When?' she asked.

'As soon as possible, but they'd like you to leave today.'

She raised her eyebrows.

'Krieselman has voiced what both you and I feel. If we're to believe in ghosts, if we're to believe that the place is haunted, then we must also accept that others believe in superstition and bad luck and jinxes.'

'And I'm the jinx?'

'Who knows?'

'There's been no directive, has there?' she asked directly. 'It's your idea. You want to be rid of me.'

'No . . .'

He was lying. Perhaps it didn't matter. Perhaps she was getting obsessed with the unimportant. Perhaps he was right and she should go.

'I'm not getting rid of you for that,' he said.

A give-away phrase. He hated the idea of her sleeping around with the staff.

'But it is you getting rid of me. It's your idea.'

'Yes,' he admitted reluctantly. 'I want to see what it's like here without you.'

'Very brave,' she said.

'How do you mean?'

'If you think I'm a jinx and somehow responsible for all

the tragedies, giving me the sack is flying into the face of danger.'

As she said it she wished she hadn't, she just wished she hadn't. A feeling, something telling her that she was asking for trouble, begging for retribution.

'We've been through too much together and I can't cope. I want Tania to take over,' Martineau explained.

'When do you want me to leave?'

'Whenever it is convenient.'

'But the sooner the better?'

'I think you should go away for a long holiday, and when everything has settled down, contact me and we'll see where you'd be best off. You have a magnificent record, but you must be disconnected from the hauntings.'

There was no point in arguing or discussing, it had been coming for months, she was surprised she hadn't got the boot earlier.

'I'll be gone by lunch time,' she said.

'Will you be all right? Have you someone to go to, or will you be alone?'

'I've got a friend or two. If not I can always find one by walking the streets.'

She said it as a joke, but it was sharp enough for him to raise his eyebrows, a headmaster disappointed with his star pupil.

'I'll come in and say goodbye when I've packed up. I presume you've told Tania.'

'Not yet.'

She left the office, drained of energy. She'd been a fool under duress. She could make all sorts of excuses of course. She was in a void. Maybe a holiday would do her good. She'd go to Greece and look for another Nikos. Or go to Japan or she'd take a trip across America. South America? The world was her oyster and she had money. She didn't have to work, not for quite a while. Maybe she should start up a PR agency of her own, with her reputation how could she fail to attract clients? Black PR she'd call it, specializing in the promotion of bad reputations.

It was just after two o'clock when she went down to her

office from her room having worked out how many packing cases she would need to clear everything from her cupboards.

Tania was behind her desk making arrangements for a Debutantes' Ball. Nikos would have enjoyed that, waiting on rich young virgins.

Tania looked up, greeted her, but no more. No comment.

'Have you seen Martineau?' Natalie asked.

'No. I was supposed to see him at half-twelve, but he's disappeared.'

'Martinet doesn't disappear. Did you page him?'

'Yes, but he's not around. He must have gone out for a lunch appointment.'

'What about reception? Didn't he leave a message?'

'No one knows where he is.'

'And no one is worried?'

'Why should they be?'

The feeling crept up her back, up her neck and under her hair making her scalp tingle unpleasantly.

'He was going to have a haircut, then a swim,' she said. 'Did you check the pool?'

'No, but I will.'

Tania rang the swimming pool, but there was no answer.

'Best ring security. I'll go down too.'

Tania gave her a look that suggested she thought she was dramatizing too much. But then Tania did not know about Nikos. Only Martineau and Derek Edgars knew about that. They were going to contain that tragedy for as long as possible.

She took the lift to the lower ground floor and turned left down the passage away from the kitchens. The hairdressing salons, the sauna, the double doors into the pungent chlorinated atmosphere of the small neat pool.

Security were already there, Edgars and his men standing over the attendant who was sitting down on a chair, very white.

Something had happened.

Derek Edgars looked over his shoulder at her and pointed at the pool. She moved closer to the edge and looked down into the blue-green water.

At the bottom, directly under the diving board, was a figure in a swim suit, a man lying crumpled at the bottom of the water, a small cloud of very red blood obscuring his head.

It was Martineau.

She stared at the macabre sight.

His body was not floating, but was curled up on itself as though in agony and implanted in the tiles, fused to the bottom.

She turned to look at Edgars, at the attendant who was quite obviously in a state of shock.

'What happened?' she asked.

'Ask him! We found him like this.'

'Why isn't the body floating?'

'Ask the body!'

She looked at the dead Martineau again. The blood was oozing from his head anew, forming a sickly pink skin on the surface of the water.

She walked slowly round the pool staring at the body. It was like a large embryo in a giant beaker of formaldehyde. Then, as she stared, one of the arms floated up and round behind his head and the whole body slowly unfolded, the neck twitched and she gasped.

The face was just a mess, without features as though it had been hit by a violent force.

The attendant looked up.

'No water,' he said. 'He dived and there was no water, and then . . . and then . . . there was.'

He stared at each of them in turn begging for an explanation.

Well there was no explanation.

She knew that. The hotel was haunted, that was all. The powers, whatever they were, could do anything they wished. They could hurl people out of windows and they could empty swimming pools and fill them up again on a whim.

All she could think of now was the likely conversation she'd have with Charmion. 'I'm afraid he's dead.' 'You slept with him, then?'

She had never done that.

She went straight up to Martineau's office, sat behind his desk and dialled Krieselman's number on the private line. As she waited for the call to be answered she swung round in Martineau's swivel chair and realized she felt rather secure, happy even, to be in charge, however temporarily.

Maybe she would ask for his job!

Krieselman's secretary answered, pretended he might not be there, eventually put her through.

'Mr Krieselman, David Martineau died an hour or so ago following an unpleasant accident.'

He asked for the details, she gave them to him, he asked if she could cope with the police and the Press, she told him she'd hold the fort.

She fielded the police and the Press with surprising ease and decided she would be ideal as a PRO in a major hospital answering enquiries about dead relatives, epidemics, accidents and all other disasters. She was a past master at feeling insensitive to other people's tragedies, putting on a concerned front without really being perturbed.

Was she perhaps being shielded by the ghosts for some reason? Helped by them?

She had prospered herself despite all the nastiness.

These thoughts, as she was ringing Charmion Martineau to tell her the bad news, made her shiver as she realized that such an idea could have a backlash and she would be next.

But there had to be a pattern and, not for the first time, she checked the photostat list of those who had died and added Martineau's name, his date of birth, profession, nationality, hobbies, peculiarities, hour of death.

There were no similarities with anyone else.

And Charmion came through.

'This is Natalie,' she said.

'I've heard.' The voice was cold and unfriendly.

'If there's anything I can do . . .' she offered.

'Oh, I think you've done enough.'

The telephone clicked. It was an accusation. Charmion definitely thought her guilty of something.

She wished, in fact, that she could be a little more emotional about Martineau, but right now it seemed she was drained of all feelings.

She pressed the buzzer and asked Tania if she could spare a moment.

Tania came in, surprised at seeing her in the commanding chair.

'Did Martineau tell you you were up for promotion before he died?'

'No.'

'Well, I was leaving, and you were supposed to replace me. Whether that still sticks or not I'm not sure, but I do intend leaving, if I'm allowed to. In fact I'm resigning.'

'Where will you go?'

'Far away.'

Tania became sweet, sat down and went into what sounded like a prepared little speech of apology. It had been hard for her, she had been frightened, the hours had been very long. She was not entirely surprised that she was being promoted and the girl collapsed into tears as she mentioned David Martineau.

Of course! Natalie now realized. Tania had been sleeping with the boss and his wife had suspected her!

She took a deep breath and sighed at her own naivety. Deception was a wonderful thing when it took one so completely by surprise and did not harm. It was even amusing, certainly curious.

They had tea together and biscuits and a whisky and felt better, then Tania said she wasn't sure whether she really wanted to go on working in the hotel now that Martineau was dead. She wasn't sure she'd be good on her own, she would much rather start again in a new place. And Natalie said she would see what she could do.

At seven o'clock a call came through from Krieselman. Would she be kind enough to attend a board meeting the next morning at nine at the company's City offices.

The sack? Promotion? Advice? Consultation?

She would be seeing all the top brass together for the first time . . . if she survived the night.

The full board was not meeting, only three of the directors with Krieselman sitting at the far end of a long table sipping coffee.

As she came in one of the directors got up to offer her a chair, an indication that they were going to be pleasant, that she was being treated with respect.

In front of Krieselman was a pile of newspaper cuttings and all the files she had compiled.

Though all four men were neatly turned out, shaven, clean shirted and smelling of aftershave, they also all looked very tired, pensive, even sad.

'We had meetings all day yesterday,' Krieselman explained weakly, 'and have come to the reluctant conclusion that we must sell the Palace Plaza.' He paused, then went on.

'We're going to close it for a full year, supposedly for alterations, for reconstruction, letting it be known that some of the problems we have had may have been due to faulty construction and electrical failures. During that time we want to retain your services to help us either sell the hotel as a going concern or as a block of service apartments. The board has decided that the Palace Plaza as such has given the company such a bad name that it is affecting business elsewhere round the world. To give you just a few examples,' he said, glancing down at a report in front of him, 'business has dropped in Paris by twenty per cent, in New York by twenty-seven, in Buenos Aires by forty! All due, we are informed, to rumours that we have been infiltrated by unstable elements, whatever that may mean.' He paused to sip his coffee, then went on. 'We suggest you take a vacation for two months from the time the hotel is officially closed, then come and work in this building for the company. Your salary and expenses will remain exactly the same.'

'When do you intend closing?' she asked.

'I understand from reception that rooms have been booked till the end of the month, so I think that the staff should be informed that we are not taking any more guests after that.'

'And what of the staff?'

'All will be paid off according to their contracts.'

'Do you want me to deal with that side, now that Martineau has gone?'

'Our accountants will deal with all those matters together with the assistant managers. All we hope is that there will be no further incidents.'

'What about the caretaker, when the hotel is empty?'

'We will hire the services of an outside security agency.'

It was the end.

As she left the boardroom, smiling politely at the directors, she got the feeling from their expressions that they feared her.

She couldn't quite put her finger on it, but sensed that they regarded her as a necessary evil. Amongst themselves it was possible that they had admitted the activities to be due to psychic phenomena and, if they connected her with them, maybe they now believed she was some sort of witch.

That is what their last looks had conveyed.

A couple of centuries back they would have had her burnt at the stake!

The winding up of the PR department was a mammoth task with which Tania thankfully helped her. Everything was put in boxes, labelled, packed away and for a whole week there was ceaceless activity in the hotel. Some of the staff worried about their future, others delighted at the unexpected redundancy payments which would allow them long holidays, others were sorry that the place had been such a complete failure due to as yet unsolved mysterious circumstances.

Natalie was aware that there was a fair amount of stealing going on. Derek Edgars reporting that he couldn't cope with the pilfering, his own staff having been reduced to two, and for the first time since starting at the hotel she told him that it actually had nothing to do with her. She had shouldered more than her share of management responsibilities over the last two years and that loyalty too was over.

On the 1st September she moved out, returning to her flat which seemed very small, very musty and very tatty. She would clean it up, refurbish it and let it at some exhorbitant price. She would give herself a week to do that then move down to her mother's cottage and give herself a fortnight to clean it up and put that up for a good let as well. A glance at her bank statement alarmed her. She had never had so much money in her life, she was rich and wondered whether she should retire, enjoy a world cruise or think in terms of settling down somewhere in the country, knowing of course that she was far too young for that and far too restless. She might seriously start a PR agency of her own though, use the money to make more money.

It was while clearing out her cupboard in the flat and emptying the cardboard box which she had raffled through for the Bible, that she found the photograph.

She had no idea that it was in her possession because it was stuck in one of the middle pages of her father's family album.

As a child she had looked through it, but maybe only once, and had certainly forgotten it.

The photograph was a family group at her father's Christening taken on a church porch. The date under the photograph in her father's own handwriting was January 4th 1919.

What made her stare at it with fearful disbelief were the three people standing behind her grandmother, who was holding the baby. There was a man with a balding head, a man with a mop of greying hair and a tall woman with a set smile of approval.

They were all younger, of course, than on the recent occasion she had seen them, but only too recognizable.

Natalie did nothing to her flat nor did she try to let it, but went straight down to her mother's cottage to sift through every possible document that might throw light on the three people.

Apart from some of her father's correspondence concerning the sale of a house in 1952 she found nothing of significance. Both her parents had deliberately tried to forget their pasts, their upbringing, relatives, their backgrounds, and had certainly succeeded in leaving little family history for posterity.

The only lead, which was a thin one, was a faded piece of blue notepaper embossed with her father's ancestral address, Charfcombe Hall in Somerset.

If it still existed someone might be living there. If someone was living there they might know about the Weir family.

She took the train to Bath then hired a taxi to take her to Charfcombe, a remote hamlet with a church, a pub, and a group of cottages. Eventually the taxi drove through some open gates and an unweeded drive to an imposing grey stone house which was half-derelict. She got out of the car, paid the driver and when the taxi had gone, she stood for quite a while alone studying the façade of the mansion.

It was part Georgian, part Victorian, she had no idea of its actual date, but the atmosphere was strange.

It was there, then, that her father had been born, that her mother had worked as a maid, from here that they had eloped one night to get married and never to return.

It was impressive, however. Much of the gardens were overgrown, the tennis court was a cage of tall weeds, the ivy was creeping up over the roof. She had missed out on this inheritance because of the snobbish accident of birth and that was hardly fair, but maybe the old place was for sale and she could buy it back, though the running costs would probably prove forbidding, not to mention the repairs.

She went up the front steps and tugged at the rusty bell-pull with little satisfaction. She walked round to the back where there was a sign of life, a washing line of male underwear and socks, cleaner windows and a back door that looked as though it could open and close.

She rang the bell, waited and eventually heard footsteps from within. The door was then opened by an elderly man wearing a clean shirt, clean corduroys, a leather tie all topped by a bright red cardigan. His brown leather shoes shone brightly.

'My name is Natalie Weir,' she started.

'Well I never!' he exclaimed, apparently delighted. 'Come in, come in.'

They went down a dark passage, up a few steps to a vast

room which had once obviously been the library but was now used as a bed-sitting room. There were a great number of books but some of the shelves which lined the walls were used to display a quantity of antiques, a collection of Coalport china, a magnificent Worcester dinner service, various large pieces of silver and three well framed miniatures.

'May I offer you some tea?' the elderly man asked.

'Yes, thank you.'

He disappeared for quite a while, giving her the chance to wander around and study everything. Most of the silver cutlery in a violet velvet-lined cabinet was engraved with the letters BW, then as she approached the three miniatures she recognized her old friends. The bald man, the white haired man and the tall woman.

'You, then, are Bruno Weir's daughter?' the elderly man said, coming back in with a large tray laden with a priceless tea set and biscuits on a silver dish.

'Yes,' she said.

'Is your father still alive?'

'Oh no. He died in 1965.'

She watched him pour out the tea carefully, tea first, milk in after, picking up the sugar cubes with silver tongs engraved *BW*.

'May I ask,' she said, taking the proffered cup from a slightly trembling hand, 'who you are?'

'My name is Adam Kelsall, I was your uncle's companion, your uncle Brendan.'

'I never knew him.'

She accepted a crisp chocolate biscuit and noticed the man's hands were silk white and that he wore a number of expensive rings on his fingers and a gold chain round his wrist.

'Your uncle Brendan inherited the estate and when he died he kindly left it to me. He meant well of course, but it was hardly a joyous gift. By leaving it to me he in fact made sure that I would remain as caretaker. It's been twenty-five years now and slowly but surely I have had to close down the rooms. In summer I sleep upstairs, but in winter I can only heat this one room.'

'You live here alone?'

'But for the cats.'

She had noticed the smell of cats but could see none around.

'There are seven in all, but they are not allowed in here because of the rugs.'

The carpets and rugs, mostly Persian, were in an immaculate condition.

'You keep the place beautifully.'

'I know,' he said immodestly. 'My life's work. I used to look after the garden too, but can no longer do so. Old age, rheumatism forbids. What can I do for you?'

She hesitated for a moment then stood up and walked over to the set of miniatures.

'These three people, who are they?'

'Who?' he asked astonished. 'They're your grandfather, his brother and sister. Aubrey Weir, Reynold Weir and Felicity Weir.'

'When did they die?' she asked.

'My dear lady, do you not know anything of your family history?'

'No. My father died when I was seven and my mother never spoke much about him.'

'I see . . .' He was pensive for a while, as though he were not sure that he should tell her, that it was his business to do so. Then he stood up and taking a stance with his back to the marble fireplace addressed her.

'Aubrey Weir was born in 1890, Felicity in 1891, Reynold in 1892. Aubrey was the only one to marry. He had four children, three boys and one girl, Brendan, Beatrice, Bruno – your father – and Bunty. Bunty was killed in the Second World War. Your father married your mother in 1958. Your mother, as you must know, was a skivvy in this house.'

He paused as though to recollect something he might have forgotten, then continued.

'Brendan and Beatrice were both to be married in 1940. A double wedding. Their parents, that is your grandfather Aubrey, his sister Felicity and brother Reynold, were in their London home on the eve of the wedding when, during the Blitz, a bomb dropped on it, killing them all. The wedding never took place, only a funeral instead.'

He went to the shelf where the three miniatures were propped up and picked up the middle one, turned it over and handed it to her. On the back was stuck a simple family tree.

'I drew that out, strangely enough not so long ago, maybe about two years ago, that is why it is so extraordinary that you should turn up. I was an orphan and had no family of my own, so I rather adopted you Weirs. Even your name is on there. The only living blood descendant.'

Natalie studied the tree for quite a while. Some of the names were familiar. She had heard of Bunty, of Beatrice, of Brendan, but she had never heard of Felicity or Reynold her great Uncle and Aunt.

'Where was the house in London?' she asked.

'Number 12 Palace Terrace.'

'Where the Palace Plaza Hotel now stands?'

'I wouldn't know dear, I haven't been up to London for fifteen years.'

Natalie handed him back the miniature, sat down and helped herself to another cup of tea.

'So out of all the Weirs, I am the only surviving member?'

'Yes,' Adam Kelsall said, looking a little uneasy.

He smiled nervously, fingered his tie.

'Were you thinking about the inheritance? It passed straight to Brendan as head of the family. Beatrice contested the will, your father didn't and I . . .'

Natalie stood up.

'I'm not at all interested in any of that,' she said, 'but I would be curious to know if this place is haunted, or if you believe in ghosts.'

'Goodness, do I look like one?' Adam asked, amused. 'I sometimes feel I look like Miss Havisham from David Copperfield. But no . . . there are no ghosts here, though memories are ghosts, I suppose, and there are plenty of those.'

'My father's family were very proud people it seems.'

'Oh indeed. Very proud. Your father bore the brunt of

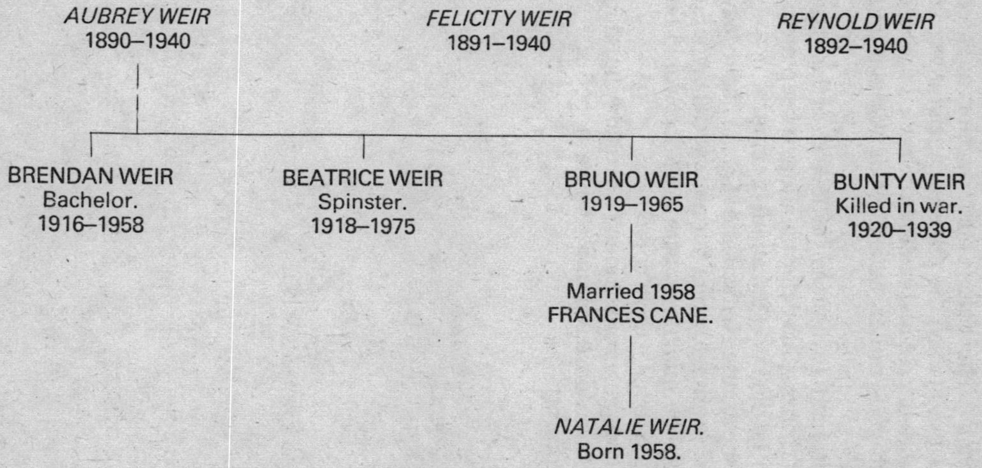
AUBREY WEIR
1890–1940
FELICITY WEIR
1891–1940
REYNOLD WEIR
1892–1940
BRENDAN WEIR
Bachelor.
1916–1958
BEATRICE WEIR
Spinster.
1918–1975
BRUNO WEIR
1919–1965
BUNTY WEIR
Killed in war.
1920–1939
Married 1958
FRANCES CANE.
NATALIE WEIR.
Born 1958.

that disease when he married your mother, and so did I when Brendan chose me as a companion after he had recovered from the 1940 shock.'

'You've lived here alone then, since my aunt died?'

'Yes. I tried to sell the place once, but it was useless. It's riddled with dry rot and can only be pulled down. The land's not much good either. Sad. No one wants it and it is very isolated.'

She listened to him as he talked of his situation, his financial distress, his determination to keep the place going till either he died or it fell about his ears.

Then she excused herself and said she had to leave, but not before asking him to grant her one special favour. Could she take away the miniatures with her? She would return them but wanted to have them copied.

Adam was generous, though it probably hurt him, he gave her the three portraits and said he hoped she would find them a comfort.

CHAPTER TWELVE

Back in London, the following morning, she had no difficulty in getting into the hotel. Though the security staff were new, Derek Edgars had been retained as consultant, knowing everything there was to know about the place.

He let her in not even asking her why she wanted to come back.

'What's it like here now?' she asked.

'Lonely. It's a mausoleum.'

She took it slowly, holding the three miniatures in one hand and visited each floor hoping for some manifestation, using the staff lift between floors, the only one now in service.

In Donald's old room she looked out of the window through which he had fallen and took a very deep breath.

'If there is anyone,' she stated in a low voice, 'if any of you are here, please make contact, somehow, I am not afraid.'

There was a rustle behind her and she turned round.

The room was quite empty.

The sun streamed through the windows, not only showing up the dust but casting her shadow very sharply on the light grey carpet.

Suddenly, as she looked down, she saw another shadow forming beside her own.

It came up very gradually as though a liquid were oozing up through the pile. It took shape clearly as a man, then to his right a woman's form appeared, then to her right another man.

The shadows swayed very slightly and she realized, looking at the four flat black images on the floor, that the ghosts were on either side of her though they could not be seen.

She put her hand out so that her shadow fingers touched one of the shadow ghosts, but felt nothing in the air.

'You are here?' she said.

All three shadows nodded.

'What do you want of me?'

The shadows swayed then, as she watched, they very gradually faded.

She waited for quite a while for something else to happen, expecting the three spirits to materialize perhaps, but half an hour went by without anything happening and she went back down to her empty office, then left the hotel.

Natalie contacted Madame Raymonda and asked her to meet her at the hotel that afternoon.

'Oh yes my dear, the atmosphere is ever so much better,' she said on entering the main foyer. 'They'll be upstairs though, won't they?'

'How do you know?'

'Who can tell? I often ask myself but never come up with an answer. A sixth sense.'

Natalie took her up to Donald's room.

'No dear. Not in here. Nothing in here. Slight oppression. I expect someone died here, but nothing special. They'll be below this floor. I'm rather like a water diviner you see.'

They went down to the next floor and the next till they reached the first.

'Here dear, over here, somewhere.'

She led Natalie to the Princes' Restaurant.

'Yes. They're here. Over here in the corner.'

Quite unexpectedly Madame Raymonda sat down cross legged on the carpet.

'I'd love to!' she said suddenly to no one. 'Thank you. I'll have yellow if I may.'

She went through a mime of playing some sort of dice game and moving a piece in the middle of a non-existent board. Her voice changed, became higher pitched, more eerie, child-like.

Natalie moved round only to realize that Madame

Raymonda had her eyes closed and was rocking herself forwards and backwards. She then spoke, like a ventriloquist's dummy, using three distinctly different voices.

'It's my turn you silly goat!'

'Is it? I'm sorry, Felicity.'

'Actually, it's my turn, Aubrey.'

'You're always cheating.'

'I'm not!'

It was a game of Ludo and it went on for some twenty minutes with other sounds in the air of doors banging, drawers being opened and closed, of people running, breathing heavily, laughing.

Then Madame Raymonda came out of it.

She was sweating and was quite exhausted.

'Oh, my dear . . . I hope you noted all that.'

'Yes. More or less.'

'Could I have a cup of tea? But not here. Let's go to that little place where we went last time.'

They did, as though the afternoon's manifestations had never happened and again the clairvoyant spoke only of her own life until she had finished her tea.

'What did it all mean?' Natalie asked.

'Oh they're children, that's all.'

'Aubrey, Felicity and Reynold?'

'Yes. You know them then? It's quite clear they're haunting the nursery they were in, reliving their happiest moments.'

'But do they want something?'

'I expect they want their house back.'

'But it was bombed.'

'I dare say.'

'Why should they focus on me?'

'Blood relation? Follow it down the line and you'll see you're connected, I expect. Some ghosts, this is not at all proven, but some ghosts can only manifest themselves through the presence of a blood relation. Blood has never really been closely examined, you know. It has all sorts of properties one wouldn't dream about. We talk of genes, maybe it's the same thing. We inherit all sorts of things from our ascendants and I believe that some ectoplasm is handed down. I mean, one hears of the Bourbon nose, of certain features being passed on in Royal families, portraits that are remarkably similar, why not some portion of the brain? The blood? You're connected to them by some umbilical thread of life, and they need you.'

'They need me?'

Oh yes. Reaching out for you they are, like people drowning, clutching at a straw. You're probably their last hope of survival on this plane, and spirits do hang on.'

'What should I do?'

'I don't think you have a choice. You have to do what they want. You could try going away, but I expect they'll bring you back. After all, now that you know you're responsible for all those deaths you can't very well allow more to happen.'

It was a terrible thing to say, but Madame Raymonda was right. Her own conscience would never allow her to leave things be, and the ghosts were playing on her conscience.

'How can I contact them and find out exactly what they want?'

'Perhaps you should just go and live in the hotel alone? You needn't tell anyone, just go and live there for a few days and see what happens,' Madame Raymonda suggested. 'There's nothing to be frightened of, you know that. You're the last person they would want to harm, and with their psychic powers at your command you could no doubt make extraordinary demands. Yes, you could make quite extraordinary demands.'

Natalie moved into the hotel secretly.

Telling Derek Edgars that she wanted to stay there for a few nights before giving up all the research, she slipped him a back-hander to keep quiet, and keep quiet he did.

She moved a bed down from one of the rooms to the Princes' Restaurant and settled there, deciding to stay for thirty-six hours. If at the end of that time she had not made further contact she would feel free to leave.

She had hardly finished making the bed when she heard an unusual noise. Straightening up she listened carefully and heard the clear sound of children laughing. They were laughing so much, giggling and screaming with delight so loudly that she started smiling herself, the sound was so beautifully happy.

Then it stopped and she heard a fearful piercing whistle, followed by a horrendous crashing boom.

Silence.

She had put her hands to her ears and she now lowered them slowly.

A bomb?

The Blitz?

Their moment of death relived?

Then they appeared, the three of them, first as reflections in the wall mirror, then as definite shapes as she had seen them before, standing close together, frightened, it seemed, of losing contact with each other.

They nodded at her, pleased that she was there.

'What do you want me to do for you?' she asked.

They stared blankly at her.

Maybe it was like a game of Ouija, like Planchette, they could only answer in affirmatives or negatives.

'You want something?'

They nodded.

'You want your home back?'

They hunched their shoulders as though expressing that they did, but only more or less.

'Certain rooms, certain floors?'

A yes.

'One certain room?'

Oh yes.

'Your nursery?'

Affirmative.

'You want your nursery back for yourselves and only for yourselves?'

They were leaping up and down joyously and kissing each other.

'You want your nursery exactly as it was?' she asked,

aware that her extraordinary intuition was perhaps being fed to her by them.

Yes! Yes! Yes!

'Can you help me get it for you?' she asked.

Nods all round.

'Then you must create a manifestation in front of certain people.'

Yes.

'Will you do that?'

Yes.

'On a definite day at a definite hour?'

Yes.

'Next Sunday at eleven o'clock in the morning?'

They nodded, looked at each other like children and jumped up and down in excitement.

She had given them permission to misbehave.

Through Krieselman Natalie invited as many directors of the hotel's company board as wished to come to experience an example of the supernatural manifestations which had led to the closing of the London Palace Plaza.

She set up a boardroom table in the Princes' Restaurant, persuaded Derek Edgars to come and help pour out drinks and decided that if the ghosts did not help her she would leave, not only the hotel itself but London and even maybe England.

It was not pretence, she had made up her mind, she believed that they knew her thoughts so that it was now up to them.

Seven sceptical gentlemen turned up on the Sunday morning and, after one stiff drink and polite conversation, they sat down to await developments.

More quickly than she had even expected, she suddenly saw Edgars freeze as he looked in the long wall mirror. The others followed his gaze.

She could not believe her own eyes.

The reflection of the room was changing very gradually, from the modern coral carpet and furnishings to the straight lines of the room, a metamorphosis started taking place.

The room narrowed, became lighter, brighter, an Edwardian nursery took shape, with doll's houses, a rocking horse, a toy theatre, an army of lead soldiers, a quantity of pretty dolls. It was like looking at a cinema screen in three dimensions and so unbelievable that Edgars went up to the mirror to touch it, but as he did so it shattered, the glass splintering outwards, cutting his hands.

Then a series of incredible occurrences followed in quick succession, chairs were hurtled across the room, the long table rose several feet and was turned over to crash to the floor upside down, the carpet moved up and down like a rough sea, the lights went on and off, there were noises of thunder, hissing, screaming, ghoulish laughter, childish laughter, finally Edgars was picked up bodily, held some six feet above the floor, then hurled by a hideous force out of the largest window, the glass shattering on impact with a deafening crack.

'You didn't have to do that! You didn't have to do that!' Natalie screamed out, horrified.

Everything stopped.

There was complete silence.

She looked at Krieselman, at the others.

They were ashen.

'Tell them they can have what they want,' Krieselman said at last. 'In exchange for a guarantee of peace.'

There was nothing else he could do, he knew that, the board knew it too and had to accept it or lose the hotel. They could tell the world that she was a witch, a medium dominated by dangerous spirits and they would put her away, which might well bring on a supernatural wrath of unthinkable dimensions. Krieselman was astute enough to know when to comply with the demands of a superior opponent.

'Carte Blanche,' he said to her, 'and good luck.'

The alterations took three months. The nursery was built and furnished according to their directions.

She decided to have her own suite of rooms on the same floor, a beautiful apartment leading into an exceedingly comfortable office, which in turn led into the nursery itself.

She was appointed manager of the hotel, and she re-employed a few of the old staff, Tania as PR, Steve as barman upstairs, several of the banqueting managers, the same chefs, the same chambermaids.

For the rest of the year she ran the place without a hitch. Whenever there were major problems she consulted her grandfather, the white haired man, her great uncle or great aunt. She put by a great deal of money, she entertained a great deal, had herself the occasional young lover, perhaps drank a little too much, ate a little too richly.

Then one day, at a banquet organized to launch the biography of a retiring MP, the three old people appeared among the guests.

'We're bored,' they explained.

She threatened to leave, but they only grinned back.

Panic-stricken, she rang Madame Raymonda.

'My dear, ghosts are like children and not necessarily bright children. They have unknown powers, can misuse them and one cannot reason with them. They have no logic, they live in a different time zone, with different values. You have done exceedingly well keeping them under control all this time.'

She went back to them and begged them to behave, but they conveyed to her that their life was tedious, that their death was tedious, that they didn't want to be kept in their room all the time and wanted to mix with people.

'Would you like to be visited?' she suggested.

Yes.

'Be good and you'll have a party every day,' she promised.

And with her endless flare for publicity, she opened up the nursery to the public, launching it with a psychic convention, blatently telling the press that the hotel was haunted, had always been haunted, writing exclusively for one of the Sunday papers a revelation of how the famous Black Hotel deaths had taken place.

No one believed her, everyone thought her an eccentric, but they flocked in all the same, to see the room, to perceive the ghosts who never appeared, to stay in the hotel so that business boomed.

The following spring she then met a man who was different to any other she had ever known. A Frenchman, extremely rich, kind and understanding, he offered her a different life away from London on the Riviera in a villa, in Paris in a mansion, in New York in a penthouse, and he listened to her story about the ghosts and believed her without having to be shown any supernatural disaster.

He convinced her that she could leave, that just one day when she was out shopping, when she was doing something perfectly normal, she could just leave by never returning to the hotel.

'We will not talk of dates, we will make no plans, I will simply expect you when you arrive,' he said, and she tried very hard not to think about him, or about a different future.

A call came through one morning from a journalist who wanted to take her out to lunch. He was a regular visitor to the hotel, always fun. She accepted the invitation and blocked off any ideas that this would be the day, the opportunity to get away.

As she went through the revolving doors however and into the bright daylight she felt quite suddenly, deep inside herself, that *they* knew and that they did not mind. What they might object to was her not saying goodbye.

She hesitated, thinking it might be a trap of some kind, but went back into the hotel, straight to the nursery and closed the door to stand there alone waiting for a contact.

She felt an extraordinary nostalgia.

She realized now that she didn't want to go at all.

She was happy here, everything was working for her, it was good, she didn't even care about the rich Frenchman.

She went to the telephone in her own suite, rang up her secretary and told her to let the journalist know that she could not make the lunch. She had a headache, needed to rest, and in fact this was true, so she took off her clothes and went to lie down on her king size bed, feeling remarkably content.

The following day she went through her usual routines, dealing with correspondence, giving orders to all the departments, coping with all the petty problems that inevitably arose.

She rang up the journalist and apologized, he suggested another date which she accepted. She wouldn't moonlight, she would stay for ever, and *they* knew.

The crisis was over.

Frenchy would have to live without her, the Riviera and all that his way of life entailed suddenly had no meaning for her whatsoever. She felt like a wife who had suddenly realized that the man she was married to was the best she could hope for and she shouldn't make plans all the time to leave him.

Then the next day she decided to go shopping to buy herself a new house gown, but as soon as she went through the revolving doors and outside on the marble steps, she felt a terrible oppression. At first she thought her eyes were clouded, then she realized it was a blanket of fog, a thick wall of it, though when she looked behind her all was clear.

Puzzled, she went back into the hotel and found everyone standing quite still, everything motionless, silent, except for her three friends who were standing at the top of the stairs in evening dress.

For the first time she heard them speak, the woman in an extraordinarily clear voice.

'My dear Natalie, welcome.'

'What's happening?' she asked, feeling a little frightened, a little unsettled.

'You don't know? She doesn't know,' Aunt Felicity said, turning to the others.

The tone was unpleasant, a superior mocking an inferior.

'Doesn't she know?' the white haired man repeated.

'She doesn't know,' the bald one explained.

And they all shook their heads in sympathy.

'Shall we tell her?' The woman asked.

'Yes. Aubrey, you tell her.'

'No, you, Reynold.'

'Actually I think Felicity should, woman to woman.'

'Well, my dear,' Felicity said coming soundlessly down the stairs, 'I'm afraid you died two days ago you see. So you're one of us now.'

She wanted to turn and run. She wanted to get away from them, far away. They were changing their faces, becoming skeletal, losing their clothes, they were going grey. And she looked at her own arms and found them very thin, the skin yellowish. She looked in the mirrors and saw four skeletons draped in white gossamer, four, one of them herself.

Then the lift doors opened and several men came out dressed in black, carrying a coffin with a funeral wreath on top of it, and behind it walked Tania and Krieselman, the members of the board and many of the staff.

'They have done you frightfully proud my dear,' Felicity said, pulling her to one side. 'I expect they're going to make even more money out of your passing away, just as you did out of us. But you won't mind. We didn't. That sort of thing doesn't matter on this side.'

She saw Madame Raymonda in the procession, carrying her cat, and both the clairvoyant and the cat suddenly seemed to look in her direction and smile with some sort of understanding.

'What did I die of?' she asked her aunt in a whisper.

'A simple little heart attack when you were asleep my dear, a little shock when you were dreaming that you met us on these stairs and that we spoke to you and that you were watching your own funeral . . . we couldn't very well let you go with that awful Frenchman, *abroad*!'

MY LOVE FOR YOU

MY LOVE FOR YOU

STELLA CASALTA

GRACEWING

First published in 2003
Gracewing
2 Southern Avenue
Leominster
Herefordshire
HR6 0QF

ISBN 0 85244 564 4

Typesetting by Action Publishing Technology Ltd,
Gloucester GL1 5SR

Printed by
Newton Printing Ltd, www.newtonprinting.com

CONTENTS

This book is dedicated to the memory of
Fr Maurus Green, OSB
of Ampleforth Abbey
who died 12 September 2001

A PILGRIM CHOOSES GOD

Places of pilgrimage are on the increase. Pilgrims who choose to foster the graces they receive in obedience to God experience, perhaps for the first time, deep intimacy with Our Lord. One such is Stella Casalta, a housewife and mother in her fifties. Until 1989 she was a Catholic, faithful to her duties, more out of fear than love. In that year she joined a pilgrimage with her close friend Joyce.

Both returned home changed people, in that their spiritual lives have entered new but different dimensions. Whereas Joyce has been given a deep love of Our Lord without any special insight, Stella has been led gradually to overcome her agoraphobia, led by Our Lord himself to undertake tasks at Mass which terrified her at first but which she has been able to perform with growing confidence.

More unusually, after receiving Holy Communion, she has been granted inner visions of Our Lord and Our Lady who give her messages concerning her family and other friends and neighbours. For example, she has been given a fruitful ministry to the sick and dying of her own neighbourhood, comforting them by assuring them of God's personal love and helping them to die well.

Other messages are for everyone in general, given to assure them of God's deep merciful love for each one.

This book contains only messages of this universal kind.

As you read, please bear in mind that Stella has a very poor grasp of English and can only express herself coherently when writing down the messages she receives. This, I suspect, may be the reason why it is not always clear which messages come from Our Lord and which from Stella as a result of convictions He has given her.

Her normal inability to write coherent English is a strong sign pointing to the genuineness of the messages in which I can find no doctrinal error.

Maurus Green, OSB

THE ORIGINS OF THESE MESSAGES

(from the writer)

I am finding an increasing love for Jesus in my heart as I open my heart more and more to Jesus as I pray. I find His love is flowing more and more into my heart. This brings a wonderful peace. Now I understand what Jesus meant when He said 'I leave you a peace which the world cannot give.' Jesus knows that I would like to bring His peace, love and hope to everyone. As I go to sleep at night I am surrounded with God's peace and love, for God's love comes through my family and friends. All these messages come pouring into my head and I know that I have to write them down to help people in the world, to comfort, help and support them and to let them know that they are not alone. Jesus loves them all very much. He is there with them, caring and feeling every pain that they are feeling and if only they can learn to offer all their sufferings up to Him, He will help them to carry their crosses. So, hand them over to Him and trust.

I pray that these messages will be read all over the world and that Jesus will be able to help you all as He has helped me.

I am
the Living Bread
come down from Heaven
for you.

HOW OUR LADY HAS LED ME TO HER SON, JESUS

Our Lady led me to attend daily Mass and to recognise the true presence at the consecration, when the bread and wine become the body and blood of Christ. This is the blood that Jesus shed for us. The first drops were in His agony in the garden, where Jesus sweated drops of His precious blood for us. Then at the scourging at the pillar, the crowning with thorns, the carrying of His cross when He fell three times, opening up all His wounds and the nailing to the cross of His hands and feet at the crucifixion – it is all here in the chalice. Even the last drop that was shed when the soldier pierced His side is here. **It is all shed for you.** It may taste like wine but it is Jesus' precious blood that He shed for you.

COME HOLY SPIRIT
Fill our hearts
with your
Love.

EVERLASTING LOVE

Come Holy Spirit and open the heart of our dear friend. Give him the courage to share his pain and sorrow. Help him to hand over the key to his heart so that through your love I may be able to help ease the pain that he has carried for years. Let him see your love and your light shine through me, knowing that it is really you, Lord, that he is unlocking his heart to.

A CRUEL WORLD

When life seems so cruel and the world has turned its back on you – do not despair, for Jesus is very close to you now. His hand reaches out for you with the love you have never known before. Open your heart for He is there waiting for you to let Him in. Open your eyes, take His hand, feel His touch and let His love flow into your heart. Know your God is with you. Do not despair. Be one with your God and He will help you carry your cross, as He carried His to Calvary. Jesus died on His cross for you so that **you** may live.

KNOW YOURSELF

Know yourself as God knows you.
Love yourself as God loves you.
Know yourself as Mary knows you.
Love yourself as Mary loves you.

Discover the new you which you have locked away, a person who is loving, gentle, kind, thoughtful, understanding, honest and caring with a love that is pure as the whitest snow. This is yourself through the eyes of your true friends.

Look deep within your heart. There you will find Jesus with His Blessed Mother, shining through your eyes, the window of your soul. Look once more. See yourself as I see you – a person who is gentle, kind, thoughtful, understanding, honest, caring, wise and with a love that is as pure as the whitest snow. This is yourself through the eyes of a true friend.

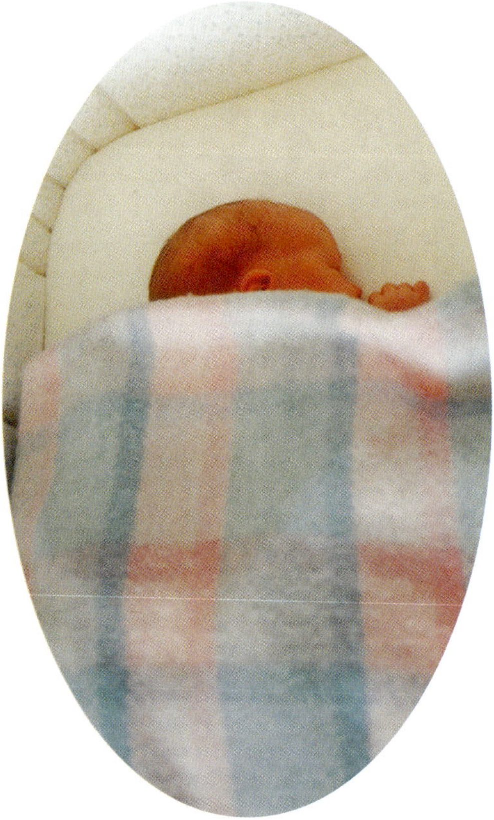

JOYS AND HEARTBREAKS OF A MOTHER

Think of the joy you feel watching your baby lying in its cot, fast asleep, so peacefully. You ask the angels of heaven to watch over your child through the night as you thank God for this precious gift that He has given to you. There is nothing so strong as the love of a loving tender mother, who cares, soothes, protects and guides her children along the right path to God. Then, one day, they are grown up, gone out into the world. What has happened to them? They have forgotten God – they do not pray any more, they do not go to church, they laugh when you speak of Jesus and Our Blessed Mother. They say it is old-fashioned to go to church. Your heart is broken. You cannot believe what they are saying. You must turn to Our Blessed Lady, for she knows what you feel in your heart. She is the Mother of Jesus, feeling great pain in her heart (as many mothers have felt) watching her son die on the cross on Calvary. Take your grown-up children and hand them over to Mary, asking her to come, soothe, protect and guide them as once you did when they were only babies. Pray to Our Blessed Lady from the bottom of your heart to guide them on the right path.

Never stop loving your children. Always show your love for them and your love for God when you go to Mass and they are not there. Take them with you in your heart. Light a candle for them, let it burn in the presence of God. Hand them over to Jesus. Trust and pray from your heart and God will save them (in His time) for Jesus cannot refuse the heart of a true and loving mother.

GIVING YOUR DAY TO JESUS

When you wake up in the morning know that you are in God's presence. Jesus is watching over you. Start the day by praying. Say your morning offering. Offer to God your day, your work, joys and sufferings. This way your whole day becomes a prayer. Walk in God's love, for He loves you very much. Bring His love to all you meet. Try to see Jesus in all people, for Jesus suffers in those who are suffering and He is joyful in those who are rejoicing. Do not judge, criticise or abuse your neighbour, for remember Jesus loves them just as much as He loves you. Ask our Blessed Lady to help you in any suffering or pain. Ask her to take it and place it in the hands of her Divine Son Jesus, to help other souls in the world, those who have lost their faith and are turning away from God. At the end of the day finish it by saying your night prayers and placing yourself in the presence of God. Go to sleep in God's love and peace.

GET YOUR PRIORITIES RIGHT

WHAT USE IS A BIG HOUSE?
WHAT USE IS A BIG CAR?
WHAT USE IS PLENTY OF MONEY IN THE BANK?

IF YOU HAVEN'T JESUS IN YOUR HEART

These are only material pleasures. If you want peace and happiness in your heart go and find God, for His love will give you the greater things, things that you only find in prayer. I am talking of real prayer, not the kind of prayer you just say, like reciting a poem and seeing how quickly you can get to the end. I am talking about real prayer! First put yourself in the presence of Jesus. Sit or kneel in a quiet place. Ask our Blessed Lady to come and pray with you. Open your heart and don't be afraid to tell Jesus how much you love Him and want to share the time with Him and His mother. When you start to pray, pray slowly, think of what you are saying. Empty your mind of all earthly distractions and just think of what you are saying and say it with love, the love you have never felt before. Now you are starting to pray from the heart.

A BEAUTIFUL SOUL FOR GOD

(On the loss of a child)

A tiny baby is a precious gift, given from God, a flower from Jesus' garden, so beautiful, so loving, so gentle, so helpless, depending on his mother's love.

We are all little children, depending on our Heavenly Mother's love. Turn to Mary in your sorrow. She is there waiting for you, to soothe and caress you. Your mother knows every pain in your heart and Mary will help you in your sorrow, if only you will turn to her, for Jesus has taken your baby and placed him in the arms of His Divine Mother to hold and caress, until the day you see him again. That day only Jesus will choose and then you will be reunited. Until that day leave your baby in the arms of our Blessed Mother and thank God that you had him for a short time. It is better to have loved for a short time than not to have loved at all. Thank God.

MUMMY AND DADDY

O Mummy and Daddy don't cry.
Wipe away your tears.
If only you could see us now,
We are so happy.
Mary has her mantle around us.
She is so beautiful.
So please don't cry,
We are safe away from the cruel world.
Mummy and Daddy, please be happy with us.

OUR MOTHER'S LOVE

Unlock your heart and let your Heavenly Mother wipe away the tears from long ago. Take your Mother's hand as a little child and let her soothe and caress you as she wraps her mantle around you, never letting you go.

DO NOT FEEL LEFT OUT

If most of your friends are saying that they have seen signs from Our Lady, such as their rosaries changing to gold while you have not seen anything, do not think that Jesus and His mother Mary have forgotten you. It simply means that they are already very close to you now, so do not feel left out. Jesus does not leave anyone out. He loves us all very much. Close your eyes and thank Him for His presence which is already in you. Remember Jesus is very, very close to you and you are one of His chosen ones, who does not need signs for you to know that He is with you.

TRUE LOVE

You have never known true love until you have felt the love of Jesus. This is the love that will never hurt you:-

a love that is so tender and gentle,
a love that is caring,
a love that is warm,
a love that is soft,
a love that is so great

that He died for you and me on the cross, not a death of peace, but a death of suffering, of scourging, a death of being laughed at and scorned, a death of enormous pain, a death of being nailed to the cross, a death of hanging on the cross for three hours. What love Jesus has for you. He underwent a death full of agony and suffering and the only thing that He was guilty of was that He loves us all so very, very much.

Stop for a few moments, ask yourself 'What do I do for Jesus? He has given Himself for me in this way. What have I done for Jesus? Do I really love Him as I think I do or is it just words rolling off my tongue?' Words are easy to say.

DO I GIVE TO HIM?

Do I give Him my love?
Do I give Him my time?
Do I give Him my prayer?
Do I give Him my Communion?
Do I give Him myself?
Do I give Him my family?
Do I give Him my friends?
Do I give Him my sorrows?
Do I give Him my joys?
Do I praise Him?
Do I glorify Him?
Would I be prepared to die for Jesus
  as He died for me?

When you know the answer, then you will know if you really love Jesus, or if you just say you love Him.

GOD'S LOVE FOR YOU

Have you stopped for a moment, away from all your material distractions, to think of God? Jesus loves you, yes you. He gave His life for you. What more could He give? How many of your friends would die for you? And yet you turn away from Jesus. Maybe you go to church on Sundays just for one hour, receive Jesus and leave in the next five minutes or even before Mass has finished and forget about Jesus until the following Sunday. Jesus is thinking about you every minute of the day and night. He loves you so much, He is waiting for you to turn to Him. Open your heart and feel Jesus' love flowing for you. He is so gentle, like a gentle breeze blowing on you with His love, for His love is like the warm sun shining on you, warming you and nurturing you. Do not turn away, take Jesus' hand. Walk with Him and you will find peace, love and hope, for He is always there waiting for you.

FEELING TRAPPED

Don't feel trapped in your sins, don't feel that your sins are so scarlet that God will never forgive you – that is saying God is a liar. All He is waiting for is for you to turn to Him and confess, tell Him how sorry you are, how much you hate these sins, because they hurt Him so much. Remember His great love for you – yes you. Remember He can see right into your heart, He knows you want to go to confession, but you may be afraid – what will the priest think of me, will he recognise my voice? Let me share an experience I had going to confession. As I started my confession I felt that I was meeting Jesus, who had been waiting for me, I could feel His love, gentleness and forgiveness. I was full of peace. I came out of confession knowing that I had just met Jesus.

So don't feel trapped in your sins, remember that Jesus is waiting for you – don't make Him wait much longer.

CHRIST HAS DIED
CHRIST HAS RISEN
CHRIST WILL COME AGAIN

In the Eucharist is the real presence – the love of Jesus

Our Lady is asking us to believe in the real true presence of her son Jesus in the Holy Eucharist. Don't just look at the host and think of it as just a piece of bread. After the consecration is when the real presence of Jesus is with us. Look at the host with great reverence and know that this is not just a piece of bread, this is Jesus, who has died for you, yes you. On Good Friday He gave His life for each and every one of us. Try to see that this is your Jesus who loves you very much. He must love you because He died for you. Thank Him, praise Him, glorify Him. In the chalice this is the true blood of Jesus, shed for us. Offer to Him all the people you love and all the people who may have hurt you, offer them now, at the consecration. Also people you may be worried about, any members of your family who have stopped going to Mass, children in danger from drugs, alcoholism, wrong relationships, marriage breakdown, a very sick person, someone dying – you can hand them over to Jesus knowing that He is really there listening to your prayers. Believe that He will hear you and answer you, not always the way you want, but the way He wants. NOT MY WILL LORD, BUT YOURS.

WHEN YOU ARE TROUBLED

('Come to me, all you who labour and are overburdened, and I will give you rest.')

Hand all your problems and troubles over to our Blessed Lady. You may feel that you are carrying a heavy load on your back, packed with all your troubles and it is dragging you down. What a relief it would be if someone were to say to you 'Let me carry your troubles just for today'. Well, that is what Our Lady is saying to you. So hand them all over to her now. She will take them to her son Jesus and He will listen to your prayers. But you must open your heart and pray from your heart, not just from your lips. Don't just let the words roll off your lips – think of what you are saying and say it from the heart.

Not my will Lord but yours.

O Mary
enfold us
in the
radiance
of Your
LOVE

DO NOT FEAR

Do not fear if you find that Jesus is going to call you home in a short time, but thank God that He is giving you time to prepare yourself for Him, for He loves you very much and has been preparing a beautiful heavenly home for you. He is waiting for you with a love that no words here on earth could ever explain, a love so great for you that He is now surrounding you with it, for He is with you now, at every moment, watching over you, drawing you into His Divine Heart. Feel His presence – give yourself to Him. Tell Jesus how much you love Him and Mary His Mother, for wherever Jesus is, His mother is there also. Ask Mary to put her mantle around you now. God is ready for you. Make sure that you are ready for Jesus and fill yourself with God's grace and ask for His Divine Mercy. Receive the Sacrament of Reconciliation and receive Jesus in the Holy Eucharist. Bind your heart to Jesus' Sacred Heart and feel His peace and love which He is showering down on you as you prepare to go home. So now prepare the soul for its final journey to meet your loving Saviour and thank God that He has given you time to make your peace with Him for He loves you very much.

FOR A PRIEST OR ANYONE PRAYING WITH OTHER PEOPLE

Come Holy Spirit, be in my heart and on my lips, that I may bring your Holy Words to these people here in this church.

YOU ARE NEVER ALONE WHEN PRAYING

Don't think that because you are alone your prayers are not heard by Jesus, for Jesus said that if two or more are joined together in prayer, there He will be in the midst of them. If you are alone then, how can Jesus be in the midst of you? Before starting your prayers sit or kneel quietly for a moment and then invite our Blessed Lady and your Guardian Angel to join you in prayer. Now ask Jesus to be in your midst, for wherever Mary is, Jesus is very close. Give your heart to Jesus and pray slowly and think of what you want to say. Tell Jesus in your own words your troubles and sufferings and offer them for your sins and the sins of the world. Yes, you can help to bring peace to the world by offering Jesus your sufferings. Tell Jesus how much you love Him. You are alone most of the time but you can do so much for your friends and the world out there, by offering everything up to Jesus. Be happy and thank God that you can do so much.

JESUS

Jesus is in my eyes.
Jesus is in my hands, reaching out in peace.
Jesus is in my mouth, receiving His precious body and
blood and giving words of love and praise.
Jesus is in my ears, listening to the troubles of many.
Jesus is in the air, in the fragrant smell of the flowers.
But most of all,
Jesus is locked away in my heart.
In every beat of my heart there is Jesus.

WORDS OF LOVE

Your tongue can say words of wisdom, words of love, words of joy, words of encouragement, understanding and help, coming to your loved ones and friends like a beautiful bouquet of roses. But your tongue can also hurt your loved ones if you speak without thinking first. It can be a whip, wounding the one who loves you so much. So, always think before you speak.

FOR SOMEBODY WHO IS DYING

Jesus take me into your heart, my hour is near. But I am not afraid as you are so close to me now.

THROUGH THE EYES OF A CHILD

I met you today Jesus, through the eyes of a child.
I looked into your eyes Jesus, through the eyes
of a child.
I wiped away your tears Jesus, through the eyes
of a child.
You saw how much I love you through the eyes
of a child.

Like a Candle
our life is consumed
before the
Face of Christ.

HOLY SOULS

November is the month we remember the holy souls, our beloved ones who have left this world and now see the glory of God. How often do we think of them? The days you spent together – does it still hurt when you think of them? Now ask yourself, 'When was the last time I prayed for them? Yesterday, last week, last month?' Those beloved ones of yours are waiting for your prayers every day, yes, every day you can help them. If only we realised the power that we have to help the poor souls in Purgatory. Their need for us to help them in their sufferings is immense. They continually appeal to our charity. The means we have at our disposal to do this are enormous, **so we must not forget them**. The day will come when **we** are waiting for prayers and the poor souls you pray for now will be praying for you in the hours of your suffering. Don't just wait for November to pray for these souls, pray every day of the year, offer up your daily work, your trials and sufferings through the day and then your work and sufferings become a prayer. Also remember the poor souls who have nobody to pray for them. It is a good and wholesome thing to pray for the dead that they may be released from their sins.

IN MY SORROW

Lord you have taken my beloved one. My heart is broken, but I know Jesus that it is only for a short time as one day we will be united again in your kingdom. My heart is weeping but Jesus I know that you have my beloved one close to you. You have taken him Lord from this world and from my sight, but I know that I can still help him. He is still with me in spirit. Thank you Lord for my family and friends, their love is helping and supporting me and I know it is your love that comes through them. I will pray for (name's) soul every day so he will soon be in your kingdom. I know he will be praying for me here on earth so I will be united with him in prayer. When I have prayed for him I can close my eyes and sleep knowing that I have helped him all I can for this day.

FINDING JESUS

Just think of one person you love the most – maybe your husband, your son, brother, father, uncle or grandfather, your mother, wife, daughter, sister, auntie or grandmother. Do you love this person enough to die for them, to give your life for them? You may say yes now, but when the time came, would you still say yes? It would be very hard, and that is for someone you love very much. Now Jesus died for us all, for each and every one of us, for the ones who love Him but also for the ones who are turning away from Him.

Just think of His great love for you. Just stop and think of this love for you, yes you. Now just sit for a moment, close your eyes, never mind what is going on around you, just think of this love completely surrounding you, like a loving mantle around you, keeping you safe, protecting you, guarding and gently guiding you. Now you must open your heart and meet Jesus – He is waiting patiently. Tell Him how sorry you are for making Him wait so long. Open your heart, now let Him in – only you can turn the key and let Him in. Now just feel that peace, that love, how quiet and gentle He is. He comes to you very gently. Meet Him, just be with Jesus, don't keep Him waiting any longer. Tell Him how much you love Him, how sorry you are for all your sins, for hurting Him – for when you sin you are hurting Jesus, just as the soldiers hurt Him when they were scourging Him and crowning Him with thorns. Why are you hurting your Jesus? Is it because you don't know Him? If you get to know Him more, you will stop hurting Him and instead you will feel His gentle love flowing for you. Jesus always has His arms outstretched to you. Go to Him, be with Him. BE STILL AND KNOW MY PEACE.

(I will leave you now, locked in the arms of Jesus.)

FOR A PRAYER GROUP

Invoke the Holy Spirit by praying to Him. Empty your mind of any troubles, sufferings and especially any hatred. Do not stop the grace that Jesus has from showering upon you. Do not block His grace by holding a grudge. Do not say 'I can never forgive that person', for God **always** forgives. God does not say I can never forgive, so open your hearts ready for all the blessings waiting to be showered down on you and your family. Don't forget that if you block these blessings, you are blocking them from your family also, your loved ones whom you really want to help. Give yourself over completely to Our Lady and let her work through you. **Trust**.

WHEN SOMEBODY IS FINDING FAULT WITH OTHERS

Stop acting like God, judging people and talking about them. Look for the good things in people and take a look at yourself, your inner self.

THE TUNNEL OF DARKNESS

Lord I am in a tunnel of darkness. I cry out to you for your loving help. Jesus, show me the way. I want to stay in your light and in your love. I do not know which is the right path. My heart yearns for you Lord. I want to stay in your love. Put your mantle around me and gently guide me. If it is not the way I would like to go I know that you will give me your strength to help me. Shine your light for me to follow, for it is your light and only your light I want. You are my true Saviour.

FAITH

Lord, my cross is so heavy today. I feel so alone. You seem so far away. I try to pray but my prayers are only words. I long to feel your presence but my heart is heavy with sorrow. I pray with faith. Oh, where are you Lord? I long for you. My faith tells me that you are near. Jesus, I offer up my cross to help to save souls in this world. Now I am one with you again, for in your passion you felt so alone – most of your friends had left you, they were so afraid themselves. You carried your cross for love of me. Now I carry my cross for love of you, Lord.

God
Bless
and
Keep
you
at this
time.

DO NOT DESPAIR

Do not despair if you feel alone and full of trouble and nobody understands you, not even your family or friends, and you have no-one to talk to, no-one who will listen to you or help you. You may feel that life is not worth living but just stop. Jesus is here, He loves you very much and if you will only try and turn to Him, you will find love and understanding and a life that is so full of pure love. Once you have found the love of Jesus you can help so many people, people who are feeling just the same as you are feeling now. So start today, turn to Jesus, talk to Him, ask Him to help you but don't forget that when you pray don't just let words roll off your lips, speak from your heart, for Jesus is there with you now, waiting for you to speak to Him.

If you have any impressions or comments about these writings please send them to:

Stella Casalta
54 Spring Gardens
LEYLAND
Lancashire
PR25 2EQ